Walk into Yesterday

Other Books by Mildred Davis

WALK INTO YESTERDAY

STRANGE CORNER

THE SOUND OF INSECTS

THE VOICE ON THE TELEPHONE

THE DARK PLACE

SUICIDE HOUR

THEY BURIED A MAN

THE ROOM UPSTAIRS

It was an unspeakable nightmare—she was in some kind of institution, and the other patients all seemed to be freaks and imbeciles. She couldn't remember her own face . . . and she was baffled by the strange scars on her arms and legs. The doctor told her that her name was Jane, that she'd been in a serious accident, that she was being taken care of by a kindly man who was her trustee and guardian. She remembered a lot of other things, too . . . but she had no way of knowing what was real and what was a product of her own fantastic dreams.

She remembered clouds, and fire, and danger, and parts of books. And a man dying. She struggled to walk into her past . . . but then a stranger appeared, and advised her that for her own safety some things were better left forgotten!

SCENE: A suburban area

WALK
INTO
YESTERDAY

Mildred Davis

PUBLISHED FOR THE CRIME CLUB BY
DOUBLEDAY & COMPANY, INC.
GARDEN CITY, NEW YORK
1967

All of the characters in this book
are fictitious, and any resemblance
to actual persons, living or dead,
is purely coincidental.

96047

To Pamela

With thanks to Dr. Thomas Uniker for all his help, and to Anne Hollyday, aged seven, for the title, *Walk into Yesterday*.

Walk into Yesterday

1

As the governor stepped out of the plane, a roar rose from the crowd and the band struck up his theme song: "From the rocky bound Atlantic to the wild Pacific shore . . ." It was like going through a door to adolescence, and when he came down the steps, the ropes strung to form a path to the terminal building (a metaphorical red carpet) were suddenly useless. Two teenagers slipped under them to shake the governor's hand, and that broke the dike.

The mob flooded under the barrier and engulfed him. Smiling sparely (everything he did was controlled and well thought out) he tried to shake as many of the proffered hands as possible. He was in his late fifties, but he looked under forty. Tall, physically fit, he had a tanned, outdoorish face, what appeared to be an open, spontaneous grin, and unusual malachite eyes. His hair had been blond once, and even now the gray was lost in the general lightness. Although the state police tried to ring him, he made the job impossible by holding out both hands so that as many persons as possible would be able to tell their grandchildren that they had touched a man who would shortly become president of the United States.

There was nothing attention-catching about the thin, nervous man with the dark Latin face. He was wearing a worn leather jacket and soiled trousers, but he was unnoticeable in the varied crowd. The governor appealed to all: the young because of his movie-star magnetism, the poor because he preached redistribution of wealth and the breakup of monopolies, the liberal wealthy because he was now one of them, the educated because he had graduated summa cum laude and was an expert at sprinkling his speeches with quotations. If there was a segment of the population missing, it wasn't noticeable. He was a "man of the people" and the people had come out to greet him.

The little man in the shabby clothing kept his right hand inside his jacket pocket as he struggled closer to the center of the crowd. Sweating, although it was November, he kept searching as though expecting instructions. Evidently he received none. He pushed a little girl out of his way without thinking, and her mother picked her up and moved back.

By now he had reached the governor, who put his hand out genially and went through his formula. "Glad to see you here today. How are you?" But then the prescription no longer worked and a new set of rules was needed because the man removed his hand from his pocket and pressed a gun into the governor's side. They were so close and the crowd so thick, no one noticed anything wrong.

The governor's eyes widened, but with surprise, not fear. What the playing fields of Eton had done for England, the gymnasium of a state university had done for the United States. With a swift movement of his arm, he knocked the weapon out of the frightened man's hand. The latter stared at him, mouth open, face wet with sweat. When the shot rang out, they were equally dumbfounded. The governor swore, grabbed his side, and then, slowly, uttering a meaningless sound, crumbled. The state policeman nearest to him stared unbelievingly for an instant and then whipped out his gun. He whirled wildly, face anguished, saw the openmouthed Latin bending to retrieve his gun, and unhesitatingly fired point-blank at his head. The little man collapsed on top of the governor.

Everything happened at once. Those nearest to the center of the cluster tried to surge back. Mothers swooped up their children, youngsters screamed with excitement, men howled questions. The state policemen tried to clear a space around the governor as they pushed aside the Latin like a sack. In the confusion no one observed the man who dropped his own gun near the Latin's hand and picked up the supposed assassination weapon. He was shoved back with the rest of the crowd by the shouting police trying to clear a path to the terminal. The members of the band, still not realizing that the chance for the presidency had oozed out of the governor's body along with his blood, continued to blare, "Great cities of importance are reached along its way. Chicago and St. Louis, and Rock Island so they say . . ."

2

On stage the elderly character actor was saying, "The squirrels have more social life than me," when she smelled something. It was vaguely familiar, haunting her like a memory of a nightmare, but she had so much on her mind she couldn't give it her full attention. She kept twisting the ringless finger on her left hand like someone unwinding a tight screw, and so many thoughts were disturbing her that this particular one couldn't squirm through.

"*Enough money to get his family out.*" Those words didn't come from the stage. She had heard them last night. And then, this morning, the news of the assassination. A chill went through her and she rubbed her arms. In all probability she was suffering from delusions and there was no connection. She shouldn't have sent the letter. How embarrassing it was going to be when they received it. When would she hear from them? Monday? Tuesday? Beside her, he took her hand and she looked at him quickly and tried to appear relaxed.

"Your maid told us to make ourselves comfortable," the second actor said, and she brought her attention back to the stage. "I never feel comfortable without a glass in my hand."

There was a titter in the audience, and she wondered what the play was about. She hoped that he, at least, was enjoying it. Taking a deep, sighing breath, she was aware of the odor again. She sniffed sharply, and behind her, someone else sniffed. In the row in front of her on the mezzanine, a head turned and she saw a puzzled face, looking everywhere. A wave seemed to pass through the theater, an aura which had no name, and yet was threatening, like the sensation, she had read once, an epileptic gets when he is about to have an attack.

"Not in front of the children," the elderly character actor said, and went into his song.

"Oh it's all right to lie, but not in front of the children.
It's all right to die, but not in front of the children.
    Make a pass
    At a comely lass,
    Act like an ass at Sunday Mass.
    Take my advice and play with dice,
    Kick the traces, go through your paces.
But not in front of the children, never in front of the children.
They're far too young."

An odd thing happened farther down the aisle on her own row of seats. A man and woman with two small children whispered to one another and then pushed the youngsters out of their seats. The latter began to protest, but the couple each grasped one and hurried them out. They didn't go in the direction of the washrooms, but toward the stairs.

At that moment she realized what the smell was.

A muscle in her cheek twitched involuntarily, and she looked around, searching for something alarming. But there was nothing to see. Unless it was alarming to have three women just below her in the orchestra get up and leave.

She had been brought up to believe that almost anything was better than losing one's head. But she was worried. She looked for the nearest exit and saw only the staircase, and it wasn't too close. She turned to look at him and smiled rather crookedly, arching an eyebrow. "I'm not worried," the eyebrow was supposed to say. And then, as though to underline that, a rough male voice from the balcony above them, growled, "Siddown. Stop acting like a bunch of morons. Siddown."

On stage, the actors could no longer ignore the rustling sounds pattering throughout the theater. The eight-year-old boy who played one of the leads was completely thrown off. Finally they gave up and turned to look at someone offstage. A heavy-set man walked on purposefully and raised his hand for attention. Behind him the curtain went down. "Ladies and gentlemen," he said firmly, "please remain in your seats. There's nothing to be worried about. Panic can cause more trouble than anything else."

"Is there a fire?" a man's voice called from the orchestra. "Tell us what's happening."

"It's completely under control. The stove in the restaurant next door—"

He never finished.

There was a hysterical scream from somewhere behind him, and as he turned to see what was happening, smoke billowed out from under the curtain. His mouth was open but no sound came from it. A thin sword of flame slashed upward and then the curtain began to curl and crisp.

"Ladies and gentlemen," he shouted above the uproar. "Please try to leave slowly. There are exits all over. There's no danger if you remain calm—"

But no one was listening. The good manners which had held her there, the inculcated conviction that it was somehow nicer to die than to cause anyone embarrassment, blazed and turned to nothing. Hell had no room for it, and it was no longer noticeable in what followed.

The scream from the stage triggered the pandemonium. She was standing, gripping his arm, but whether or not he was saying anything, she couldn't tell. The smoke filled the theater now and it was getting almost impossible to breathe. She could no longer see the stairs, and in any case, she couldn't move. The aisles were clogged with humanity. The man who had shouted "siddown" was still trying valiantly somewhere above her to restore order, to turn the panic into something which would retain the semblance of civilization, but it was too late. Even she, civilized to the nicest degree, found herself fighting a desire to claw, scratch, tear her way to freedom, escape the seething heat beginning to pour up from below, reach the blessed sanctuary of

the streets. She had never before felt so desperate a desire for
anything as she now felt for the sight of the sky, for a lungful
of sweet air, for freedom from the terrible crush of people. The
aisle was a mass of fighting, struggling arms and legs, curses,
screams, terrified faces, open mouths, staring eyes. A father held
a child above his head and tried to kick his way through; a young
man, gripping the arm of his girl, looked down helplessly, considering their chances if they jumped; two elderly people tried
to climb over the seats and the woman fell, evidently having
broken something while the man tried to get her to stand.

She was choking and sputtering as the hot smoke filled the
theater, rising toward her. She could see nothing at all now and
wouldn't have known in which direction to run even if she could
have gotten free of the crush around her. A reek of something
unspeakable, something much worse than burning wood, singed
her nostrils, and a sudden roar filled the building as with a sputtering crash a part of the wall crumbled. Two people were
buried under the broiling chaos. She saw the woman's foot sticking out from under the rubble, and it moved with a crazy life
of its own as it kindled before her eyes.

The fear was uncontrollable madness now. In the packed
mob she saw a man push down an elderly woman and the woman
disappeared as though under a wave, never to reappear. The
roar of the flames blended with the screams which rose to the
most unbearable crescendo. She saw that the father and his child
had reached the wall and the child's face was contorted with
terror. Just then the wall seemed to open behind them. At one
moment it was solid and then it was without substance, a liquid
flame. The man's mouth was open, but any sound he might have
made blended with the others around him, and it was like watching a silent picture. The child tried to fight free, but the father
must have felt it was better to hold on, and they both went down.
As they disappeared, their faces seemed to become transparent,
the flames embracing them, turning them into its own substance.

She turned for a last look at him, knowing they were going

to die, and at that moment the world seemed to give way beneath them. There was no longer anything to stand on. Inflamed with terror, she struck out, without knowing whom she was struggling against. She screamed as the torrid, blazing heat reached her cheek. As the mezzanine gave way, she tried to hold on to him, but she felt him wrench free, and at the same moment, something dug into her arm. She couldn't see, and the screams rose to one summit of piercing, inhuman sound. She turned into a simmering torch of agony as the floor fell away from beneath her, and she went down, down into the inferno.

3

The sun filtered through the naked branches of the trees, tracing a pattern of spidery shadows on the green coverlet and speckling the yellow flowers in the vase. A sprawling, unpruned rosebush, just beyond the French doors, still had last year's dried petals on it. The maple tree, however, was studded with the barest suggestion of new buds, like a nubile eleven-year-old. Someone had turned on a tap and she heard the gentle drip of the water interlaced with the voice saying, "There is no such thing as standing still, you know. You go up under your own power, or you're pulled down by gravity."

He was a slight man, with a narrow, lined face, and he was always making statements like that. She suspected that he was a frustrated writer, although she knew, of course, that he was the doctor. He was wearing a wool pullover over an open-necked shirt and badly fitting gray slacks. Despite the lined face, he appeared to be in his early thirties.

Sleepily she said, "I know how to stand still. I let the uh—" She turned to him trustfully. "I lost the word. It floats in the sky."

"Clouds."

"Yes," she said happily. She liked to recapture tenuous words. "I let the clouds carry me."

"Clouds carry only light weights. You're not a light weight."

How did *he* know, she wondered. Well, of course, they had been having these desultory conversations for a long time. How long? She wasn't sure. It was so hard to concentrate. Days? Weeks? Sometimes she had that dream again, the one about being back in school and wandering through the long, dark corridors, trying to read the numbers on the doors. She could never quite see them. And then she would try to consult her schedule and that would be blurred too. Suddenly it would be exam time and she had never attended a class or opened a book. She would have to answer for a full semester's work without one idea of what it was about. She felt that way now when he began asking her questions. Her mind would become addled and she would be full of tension again.

It was much pleasanter to drift. She let the air currents carry her away from the doctor, feeling herself moving gently through wisps of nothingness, past the thin, intertwined branches of the trees that parted to let her sift through unscratched. The clouds —no matter what he said—lifted and held her, their arms damply caressing her face. She wished he wouldn't be so earnest, so conscientious about bringing her back to earth. It was such a dirty world down there, while up here . . .

She came down with a bump and stared at something in the doorway.

It was no taller than a large doll, but there was nothing doll-like about it. It was thick and deformed, beginning with a huge head, attached apparently without benefit of neck to a hunched back, and diminishing to a shapeless body, short legs, and tiny feet. The round idiot face was topped by a few strands of oily hair, and it had small slits for eyes, a large shapeless nose, and a good-natured, smiling mouth. It was grunting and keening.

She shrank back on the bed as the thing approached, waving a cane it evidently used to help it walk. The cane lifted, and she whispered, "Go away. Please go away." She tried to remember a name to call when she needed help, but it eluded her. She was aware of an amorphous fear that attached itself to so many of her waking moments, that made her shy away from so many threads of thought: Was it possible, could it be conceivable that she herself resembled that creature?

The dwarf, which she now saw was female because it was wearing a dress, came closer, waving its cane and jabbering. In its free hand it held a sheaf of discarded papers, like the scraps a child might collect.

"Somebody!" she called out. "Somebody!"

A woman appeared in the doorway. She wore a nurse's uniform, and she was a mulatto with red hair. One of her eyes was off center. "What's the matter?" she asked in a soft, consciously genteel voice.

Of course she recognized her. She had always been here, but at the moment the name escaped her. "Oh please—make it go away."

"Who? Bonnie?" Surprised, the nurse looked down at the dwarf and swished her hands in a broomlike movement. "Shoo, Bonnie. Scat." The thing hesitated, jabbered, and then lost interest. Using the cane, it hobbled away on its tiny feet.

"Gib was with me in the market one day," the nurse began. Everything reminded her of her small nephew, Gib. "And we saw this Mongolian idiot. It was the most embarrassing thing. In a very loud voice—"

The clouds lifted her again and took her away from the voices and the sights and the memories. They turned from yellow to white to gray as time moved on. Sometimes they were a fiery orangey red which she didn't like, and sometimes a cool, blue purple which made her sad. During the days, the light wasn't as watery any longer. It became yellow and strong, and outside the French doors, the little buds grew rounder, bursting with secret promise.

She was in a wheel chair with a blanket entwined around her feet. The sun filtered onto her face, warming it. Something heavy rested on her chest, but when she tried to lift her head to see what it was, the effort exhausted her. The threadlike dreams wound themselves endlessly around her brain—a sensation of falling, of twisting down a tunnel, feeling the air rush past, unable to stop. It was like being born, a process which when once started was irreversible—you had to follow through to the end. There were faces hovering over hers. Not whole, but half faces, eyes and foreheads exposed, noses and mouths hidden by masks. She was in a pit and they were all peering over the edge. And everywhere was that smell—the pungent odor of something terrible.

She drifted away.

A man was cleaning the mulch and winter debris out of a garden bed, but he had his back to her and she paid no more attention to him than she did to the tree. He was part of the background. Another man ambled by, walking unsteadily and smiling foolishly at a private, slightly embarrassing joke. That one was called Dick, she knew, and was pleased that she could remember. Or was it Richard?

She felt a tickling sensation on her chin. It was an ant and she brushed it off.

On her chest was a stack of folded newspapers. She took her sweatered arm out from under the blanket and lifted one. But her eyes were distracted by the sight of her own hand. Did that belong to *her*? She glanced upward to the shoulder to make sure it was attached. The skin was dry and flaky and the nails cut short in a straight line. On the wrist was a wrinkled scar, fish-belly white and shiny. As a child she had been burned and she had had that shiny white skin afterwards. But that burn had been on her elbow. The memory came as a shock. She felt herself being pulled down again, away from the warmth of the sun and the green fields stretching off into the distance, and the tiny flies whirling and tumbling in the air. She made a tremendous effort not to go back into the darkness.

The newspapers were all shapes and sizes. What a lot of them she had collected, as though she had been trying to catch up with something. Snatches of print caught her attention: " . . . automobile executive stood before a New York audience of three hundred salesmen and told the story about 'grandmother's new car.' Not only did she want advanced styling . . ."

Or: ". . . the commercial theater is dying, television is corrupting everything it touches, the dance is bankrupt, actors are out of work, orchestras and operas are ridden with deficits . . ."

"Things are rough all over," she said aloud. The man who

was gardening turned, startled. But she looked at him blankly and he went back to work.

Something else crossed her line of vision. Another one of the inhabitants of this—this—what kind of a place *was* this? How many horrors did it contain? This particular one was in a wheel chair and it was so thin it might have been a skeleton lightly clothed in skin. Its head rested on its chest and it was curled up and seemed to have no life of its own, except that the claws that emerged from the sleeves of the coat were grasping the arms of the wheel chair. It was as though whatever it was expected to go hurling through space. It was probably female because it had long hair.

"Oh God, where am I?"

This time the gardener didn't bother turning as the words burst from her mouth. They vibrated on the air like discordant musical notes and they brought forth a universe full of ugly possibilities. Where am I was replaced by *What* am I? The fear of the answer nearly choked her. She sat up and the newspapers scattered. Automatically she reached out and caught one.

It had a large picture of a crowd of people. She had no idea why they should be on the front page, and she didn't care. She had caught sight of the date. For some reason the newspaper was dated ahead, about five months ahead.

The thought lay dormant for a moment, quivering and shimmering. And then it began to grow. It grew to monstrous proportions. Was the newspaper ahead or was she *behind?* Could she possibly have misplaced five months?

The dizziness, the familiar dizziness, attacked her, and the sudden blackness in front of her eyes made her put her head back. The doctor had been right all along. The clouds would no longer hold her. She had to come down and find out.

4

"You," she said hesitantly, "the gardener."

He continued heaping the mulch into the wheelbarrow and she wasn't sure whether or not he had heard her. Perhaps he was accustomed to ignoring the patients.

She wheeled herself closer. "Please! I'd like to talk to you."

He straightened slowly. He was tall and stooped, but when he turned, she could see that he was younger than he had appeared from the rear.

"Come here, please," she said.

For a moment he hesitated, and then, reluctantly, almost warily, he approached. He watched her as though expecting violence. "I've got a lot to do," he muttered.

"What's the date?"

Before he could answer, they were both distracted by the sight of a woman, staggering and jogging like a puppet with an alcoholic pulling the strings. She seemed about to fall with each step. Tall, angular, ugly, she stopped in front of the wheel chair and said, "See my letter? My brother writes. Sends letters. Money. Lots of presents. Give me presents all the time. My bracelet—pretty. Lots of cards."

"Go away, Beth," the gardener said. Then, "What did you ask me?"

"What's today's date?"

He told her.

"You're sure?"

"Of course I'm sure." He examined her covertly, as though searching for a sign that she was making fun of him.

"I don't understand," she said to herself. Then she noticed that his eyes were on her legs. The blanket had slipped. She looked too, and although she was wearing stockings she could see the marks—postage-sized cutouts as though pieces of skin had been pinched off. "Wh—when can I see Dr. Stires?" she asked, to distract his attention from her legs.

"He comes in the afternoon. Never in the morning."

"You mean there's no— Doesn't he live here?"

"What for?"

"Well—for looking after the patients, that's what for. For treating them."

He glanced at Beth. "Whom should he treat? *Her?*"

She followed his eyes and then her own dropped. She was sure his contempt spilled over on all of them, herself included.

"This isn't a place for treating people," he went on. "They're taken care of. That's all."

"But then who takes care of them?" She hesitated, feeling she wasn't being honest. "Us," she amended.

"Gillian," he answered, and went back to the flower bed.

Of course she knew who Gillian was, but she couldn't sort out the face at the moment. She tried reading the newspapers— it was like having been placed in another century. The names meant nothing.

"Time for lunch, Jane," a woman said briskly and she opened her eyes. It was a dark-skinned, dark-haired woman, heavy-set and short. Briskly she began wheeling her toward the house.

"Where's my nurse?" Jane asked. "Uh—Zee?"

"Zee? It's her day off. You know that."

She hesitated a moment. Then, taking a chance, she asked, "Who are *you?*"

The woman's eyes widened and she shook her head. "Not again," she groaned. "I'm Gillian. Try to remember this time."

It would be better not to ask so many questions. How could she have forgotten Gillian? Someone had once told her that instead of asking so many questions, she ought to observe and find out for herself. Who had told her that? Where had the thought come from? But the opaque window slammed shut and the view beyond was cut off.

They went up a small ramp into the house, and it was chilly after the sun. The rooms were large and gloomy, and she suppressed a shudder. Waiting for her eyes to adjust, she made out what appeared to be reception rooms on either side of the staircase, and a number of larger rooms with flexible functions, judging from the scattering of card tables, chairs, couches, a television set and piano.

It was like entering a wax museum. Evidently everyone ate at the same time, patients and staff alike. There was the dwarf, Bonnie; the shuffling one who always seemed embarrassed, Dick or Richard; the scarecrow in the wheel chair, Helen; the puppet-like one who always spoke about her brother and his gifts to her, Beth; and a small, thin, aristocratic-looking woman who spoke to no one. Interspersed with them were Gillian, her daughter Adeline who cleaned, the cook and her husband, and the gardener. Everything and everyone seemed distorted and blurred, figures melting and blending into one another. Sometimes she would catch sight of an expression, a piece of clothing, a smile which reminded her of a former existence or a nightmare. Then she had the sensation of looking into the mirrors at the amusement park where nothing was focused properly. It was hard to know what was real and what unreal, what alive and what a representation of what had once been alive, what the way it appeared, what thrown out of kilter by the mirror, what was normal, what abnormal, what had really happened and what only seemed to have happened.

House of mirrors. Odd, she didn't remember ever having asked for a mirror. She had no idea what her own face looked like. One would have thought that was the first thing she would want to know. Fearfully she wondered what further shock awaited her.

She looked down into her soup, as though it were a clear pool in the forest, but it sent back no reflection. Next she tried the spoon, but there she could discern only a vague oval, recognizable as a face, but without distinguishable features. When she glanced up, she found both the gardener and the cook watching her, and hastily she began drinking her soup. There was a babble of conversation around her, if conversation was the right word for what spewed forth from those poor destroyed brains. Her attention stepped daintily around the babble, like someone walking through a street full of sewage, for fear of soiling her own precariously balanced mind.

"It's true," Gillian said to her. She looked up, startled, not knowing what the woman meant. Smothering a question, she awaited further enlightenment.

"I mean what Beth was saying. About her brother being the headmaster of a boy's school."

"Oh?" she asked cautiously.

"Yes. She comes from a very good family. So does Marlene." She nodded at the small, aristocratic woman.

"Then—but what happened?"

"You mean with Beth? Oh—well, you know. It can happen everywhere. It was a birth injury, the doctor thinks. But you can't really tell, because the records weren't so good in those days. To tell you the truth, they were never sure if it was congenital or they were born with it."

It never occurred to her to correct Gillian's mistaken idea of what congenital meant, but she was pleased that she understood something Gillian didn't. She was also pleased that a supposedly normal woman considered her well enough to discuss the other patients with her.

The chicken was good, and she felt hungry, as though she hadn't eaten in years. For dessert she ate a caramel pudding with cream on it and then she had coffee. Afterwards Gillian wheeled her outdoors to the annex, past the French doors and into her own room, where she helped her into bed for a nap. "Will I ever walk again?" she asked as though the question had never seemed important before. "What's wrong with my legs?"

"Sure you'll walk again," Gillian said heartily, and before she could ask anything further, went out.

She settled back, shutting her eyes and trying to call forth images, pictures, words, anything. She had all the time in the world, and it was sinful not to use it. For a while there was nothing but the jumble of faces in the dining room. One of them seemed vaguely familiar but she had no idea which one it was.

Could it have been Richard, the smiling one? Somehow she didn't think so, and yet, something about his light blue eyes and ruddy skin . . .

There had been another face like that once, but the eyes hadn't been blank. They had been filled with warmth, love. She had a sensation of being protected; she could almost feel a large hand covering hers. Someone was telling her something.

She moved restlessly on the bed. She was trying to remember words, but instead of sound, there came an odor, a peculiarly pungent odor, not flowery but connected with pleasure. Animals! That was it. She had been at the zoo, and the man with the blue eyes—her father. Of course. All animals fascinated her, but this one particularly because it came from the other side of the world. A kangaroo. A voice saying, "Yes, every day. You're to wash your hair every day—I won't have the smell of horse in your hair."

But that was a different voice, feminine, and the time and place had shifted. Anonymous the Third—her gelding. She had once had her own horse. Deep brown—no, wait, who was the woman? It had to be her mother. Why couldn't she summon a face to go with the voice?

She moved and turned as though she couldn't find a comfortable spot on the bed. Every nerve tingled unpleasantly. She wanted . . . but she didn't know what she wanted.

On the shelf near the bed were her radio and several books which had apparently come with the room. She took one. *David Copperfield.* She had no trouble recalling a vague outline of the plot, a fool of a mother, a stepfather, the Aunt whatever her name was . . .

"It was the best of times, it was the worst of times . . ." No. That was *A Tale of Two Cities.*

There was a sick sensation in her stomach. Evidently a nerve had been touched. What was there about *A Tale of Two Cities* to upset her? Perhaps she felt like the father—what was his name?—buried alive in One Hundred and Five, North Tower. No, something else.

Echoes. The sound of footsteps, the tread of tiny feet. "Let greater echoes resound, the young mother at the cradle side could always hear those coming."

She leaned back and shut her eyes, staring dully at the window. Her head had begun to ache. "Headlong, mad, and dangerous footsteps to force their way into anybody's life, footsteps not easily made clean again if once stained red, the footsteps raging in Saint Antoine . . ."

Odd, what memories she had. Imagine remembering all that. Saint Antoine. What footsteps in *her* life had been stained in blood?

She was no longer trying to remember, but the words came anyway. ". . . loudly echoing footsteps of Saint Antoine echoed through the Paris streets in mid-July, one thousand seven hundred and eighty-nine . . . Keep those feet far out of her life! For, they are headlong, mad, and dangerous; and in the years so long after breaking of the cask at Defarge's wine-shop door, they are not easily purified when once stained red . . ."

The carpet had been red. She had gone in and he hadn't heard her. None of them had heard her. Fool hadn't locked the door after the last one had arrived. Voices from the other room. Some quality in the voices had made her step cautiously across the carpet. She had stood in the dark and listened intently—

"Hi," the doctor said, coming in after a perfunctory knock.

She blinked stupidly, her inner eye still intent on the blood-red carpet, but then his presence made it vanish. She was back in the room with the night stand, the easy chair, the closet, the

twelve inches of classical reading and the sun slanting in. The
sensation of nausea was gone.

"Were you sleeping?" Slender, his narrow, pleasant face somewhat haggard, his body encased in apparently the same ill-fitting
pullover and slacks, he sat down with a sigh.

"Not exactly."

"Not exactly?" He took out a pack of cigarettes and offered
her one but she refused. "What does that mean?"

Instead of explaining, she asked, "Did I smoke once?"

"I don't know."

"Is this all you do? Take care of the sanitarium?"

"No, I have a private practice. My uncle left me this place."

"That sounds rather odd."

"No, not really. He ran it for about forty years and when he
died, well, I couldn't simply abandon his patients. Where would
they go?"

"It sounds so lausual."

Gently he asked, "Lausual?"

"Oh—isn't that a word?"

"No."

"Oh, I know," she said with relief. "I mean casual. Isn't it
rather casual to leave you a sanitarium full of uh—us? Suppose
you weren't interested?"

"I had no choice. I was his closest relative. I thought at first
I'd simply keep it going until well—the last patient was gone.
But then you—I know your guardian and when he asked me—"

"My guardian?"

"Yes. When he asked me—"

"Who is he? What's he like?"

"His name is Howard Chalmers. He was apparently a friend
of your family's and he asked me to let you come here. You see,
you were out of your coma and had been released from the hospital, but you were still—he needed a place like this. You had
your own nurse so you weren't any problem to me."

"May I see a mirror?"

"You're really chipper today, aren't you?"

"How do you mean?"

"You're full of beans—alert, curious—it's a good sign."

"How long have I been sick?"

Completely relaxed, he leaned back in his chair with no hint of pressure or hurry in his attitude. "Quite long. Depending upon how you look at it, of course. Compared to some of our patients—"

"How long?"

"Tell me what you remember."

"Nothing. That is, quite a lot, I suppose. I mean I can remember how to talk. And I was just remembering parts of *A Tale of Two Cities* when you came in."

"What's your name?"

She shut her eyes, oddly embarrassed, as though she had committed a social error. "Gillian calls me Jane."

"And your surname?"

She stared into his kind eyes and waited, hoping he would help, but he simply smoked and waited.

"I hate games," she said finally. "Please tell me about myself, what happened, everything."

"Your name is Jane Wallcutt. You were in an accident—"

"What kind of accident?"

"You don't remember it at all?"

"No." She had a sudden thought. "Did my father have a ruddy complexion and blue eyes?"

"What?"

"I think I remember him. That is—it *might* have been my father. Did he have blue eyes? Does he?"

"He's dead and I have no idea."

"Oh. Never mind. Tell me about the accident."

"You fell."

"Fell? You know I think I fell once before, when I was a little girl. I seem to—I think I had a memory lapse then too."

"Did you?" he asked with genuine interest. "Tell me about it."

"Well—I—I feel so confused. I'm never sure if something happened or if I dreamed it. I think, I think my father was playing a game with me and I think I fell—and then I couldn't remember. Oh, let's forget that. Tell me about the accident."

"You were hurt quite badly."

"You mean my legs? My brain? What about my face? Oh yes, before I forget, please get me a mirror. I seem to be jumping from one thing to another. I feel sort of uh nervous today—will you get me a mirror please?"

"Certainly." Casually he got up, snuffed out his cigarette in a china plate on her night stand and went out into the hall. It seemed to take a long time. As the seconds ticked by, she began to be afraid that he had simply left in order to avoid giving her the mirror. At the same time, an intrinsic trust in him made her discard the idea. "Doctor!"

He returned immediately, as though her voice had triggered his resolve. She heard his step in the hall and the door opened. In his hand he held an eight-inch oblong mirror he had evidently just removed from the wall in the corridor. It was still attached to a wire and it was dusty. Without a word, he handed it to her. She didn't look at it immediately, but instead at him. He smiled reassuringly. Finally she lifted it. It was of poor quality and had streaks in it. She had to bring it quite close before she could see herself.

5

It was an odd sensation looking at one's own face and not remembering it. It was pretty, at least at first—narrow, with prominent cheekbones and large brown eyes, with only a slightly too
prominent chin marring it. She couldn't see it too well and she
brought the mirror even closer.

At closer range it wasn't quite as smooth. Although they were
faint, she could detect lines which she couldn't understand. They
were where lines should go anyway, like the crevice on her neck,
but they seemed to be scars.

"What happened to my neck?"

"It was injured in the accident. Your larynx—"

"I'm still confused. How long ago was the accident?"

He hesitated and then shrugged. "November."

She repeated it slowly, as though only by hearing it said aloud
a number of times could she absorb the knowledge. "November
. . . and now . . . it's March, isn't it?"

"Yes. Of course you're getting better every day. You weren't
in an actual coma for more than three weeks."

"Three weeks! I—sometimes—I, oh, I wish I knew what was
a dream and what was true. I can see masked faces—"

"That's probably a true memory. You saw a lot of doctors after
you came out of the coma—before you came here."

"Did I see other people too—I mean do I have uh—sevjes?"

He was puzzled. "Sevjes?"

"You know—people who belong to me—who are my—"

"Oh—relatives! No. No one who is close to you anyway. You're
not married, and your mother and father are dead."

"No brothers? Sister?"

He shook his head.

"Did *anyone* visit me?"

"Oh yes. Friends and your guardian. Your guardian is your trustee too. He's known your family for years. He was the one who signed—who gave the surgeons permission for whatever was necessary."

"There's so much I want to know. What friends came? Who are they? What's my guardian like?"

"Take it easy. You can't cram a whole lifetime in an hour."

"Oh please don't leave yet. Will I ever walk again?"

"Certainly. Don't worry about that. There's no real reason for you not to walk right now. It's just that you've been bedridden so long. And of course, there was the shock—"

"What are the marks on my legs?"

He glanced at them and then away, taking a deep breath. "They had to graft tissue from the anterior part of your thighs for your face. It's called a pinch graft. They use forceps to pinch up the skin and then they graft it where it's needed. The bits and pieces grow together. The scars on your thigh will remain like that, I'm afraid. It was your face which was important."

"What happened to my face?"

Cautiously he said, "Uh, it was pretty badly hurt. There was uh damage and it took a number of operations. The scar tissue had to be cut out. We'll discuss it at more length some other time."

"Why can't I remember anything? Why do I get my words mixed up?"

"You had a head injury, you know. You're suffering from amnesia, but I'm sure it will clear up in time. The human brain is one of the most complex—"

"How badly was my brain damaged?"

"You were very lucky. I've seen cases of falls where—well, anyway, in your case you had a severe concussion. You were in a coma for three weeks, and there was some hemorrhaging which led to the swelling of brain tissue—anyway, it clears up very gradually. The intercranial bleeding causes increased pressure within the brain, and this pressure impairs brain function."

She seemed to have lost the thread of what he was saying. Picking up the mirror, she examined herself again. Makeup or time or a tan might disguise the imperfections. Comparing herself to the women she had seen so far—Gillian, Adeline, the cook, the nurse—she was a raving beauty. "There's a nail over there on the wall—could I keep the mirror?"

"Certainly." He hung it up.

Without trying to trace the train of thought, she asked, "Are you married?"

Smiling faintly he said, "No."

"Why not?"

"I've been too busy answering questions." He started for the French doors and opened them.

"I wish you wouldn't go. Do you think I ought to have a uh —the kind of doctor who can help me remember?"

"A psychiatrist?"

"Yes. Do you think I ought to have one so he can tell if perhaps what's wrong with me isn't all physical?"

He looked at her quizzically. "What makes you ask that?"

"I don't know—I—just feel—"

"Well, we'll see."

He went out through the French windows and stopped to talk to one of the patients. She could hear the change of tone as he switched into a light, meaningless patter. At least he didn't talk that way to her, she thought gratefully.

Jane Wallcutt. What had happened to her parents? Why couldn't she evoke the most tenuous memory of a loving face, a voice? But she had—the ruddy-faced man with the blue eyes—

Outside in the hall there was a slight scuffing sound. What kind of monstrosity would this be, she wondered apprehensively. At least it wouldn't be dangerous. Certainly they wouldn't allow them all this freedom if they were dangerous. Or were there hidden rooms, cellars or attics, which enclosed subhuman, crawling growling creatures which could rend and destroy, which might escape?

She saw the door being pushed back without any visible
agency. For a moment she did nothing and then she opened her
mouth to call out just as a small, nondescript dog came in.

"Oh," she gasped. She waited to get her breath back and
then she leaned over the side of the bed. "You—come here." The
dog looked at her inquiringly, and she patted the bed. Instantly
he jumped up beside her, all loose ends quivering. She pulled
him into her arms, and although he smelled dirty, she hugged
him to her face. He began licking her and pushing his head
against her neck to make sure she didn't stop. Something achingly familiar about the curve of his body brought on another
memory. Once, long ago, she had hugged a small object like
this—she must have owned a dog. Perhaps if she could evoke
an image of the color and breed it would lead to something
else, show her another bend of the road. But instead she caught
sight of the reflected branches of the trees in the mirror the doctor had hung on the wall.

> *And moving thro' a mirror clear*
> *That hangs before her all the year,*
> *Shadows of the world appear.*

It was odd how consistently she remembered written words
instead of events. She had been searching her mind for a small
soft body, a sensation of love which made her chest ache, and
she had come up with "The Lady of Shalott." Perhaps it was a
warning. What would happen if she too got sick of shadows
and went out on the river? "Till her blood was frozen slowly
and her eyes were darken'd wholly . . ."

Zee came in, bringing back the world. She was dressed in a
smart green wool suit, her hair was in a turban, and she looked
quite chic. She caught Jane's eyes on her and, misinterpreting,
said, "Your guardian thought it would be all right for me to wear
your things. The older ones, I mean. You were—you know—
it seemed a shame to waste them."

Jane felt an odd shock, a twisting of the viscera, as though she had had a glimpse into the future and were attending her own funeral. It could so easily have been a funeral if it hadn't been for a slight chance. While she had been vegetating, a useless, mindless object, requiring endless care, the survivors had been discussing the division of the property. Aloud she said, "It's perfectly all right about the suit. You may keep it. I didn't recognize it, you know."

"You didn't?" The odd eyes narrowed and shifted quickly. Again Jane felt afraid. Perhaps she shouldn't have allowed Zee to know that she couldn't identify her own clothing, because now she might take anything. For the first time since she had regained full consciousness, she was submerged with the recognition of her own helplessness. She felt impotent; at the mercy of Zee, of all the creatures who inhabited the sanitarium, of the unknown trustee, even of the doctor.

"—looked at the sky and said, 'See, Auntie Zee, God is writing!' Isn't that cute?"

"I'd like to meet your nephew some day," Jane said and was surprised to know that she meant it.

"Would you?" Zee asked excitedly. "Maybe I could bring him back when I go home on my day off and keep him here a week."

"We can ask the doctor."

Zee went to her room to change into her uniform and then she helped Jane to get ready for dinner. Pushing the wheel chair outdoors, she said, "It isn't time yet. Do you mind if I talk to Gillian for a while?" Without waiting for permission, she left her patient in the garden, which was pleasantly warm, and hurried to the kitchen.

Looking for companionship also, Jane wheeled herself down the path. The yard man was carrying rubbish from the toolhouse to the incinerator, and anxious to talk to anyone who was normal she said, "Good afternoon. I didn't realize there's so much to do in gardens so early in the year." She detected a note of anxiety in her voice which reminded her of lonely elderly people she must have known in the past.

Before he could answer, Bonnie appeared, evidently having trailed him, and removed one of the bits of paper from the heap in his arms. He shooed her off. He was as easy with her as the doctor was, perhaps, Jane realized, because he felt no kinship with her. If she herself had been perfectly normal, she could feel easy with Bonnie too.

"Oh—I'm just cleaning up. And I've started some flats in the greenhouse. The doctor likes lots of cut flowers around. It makes it cheerful for the visitors." It seemed to her that there was a trace of dryness in his voice when he mentioned the doctor.

"Do they get many visitors here?" she asked quickly so that he wouldn't go away. She wondered what made a man of between thirty and forty, who sounded educated, work as a gardener.

"Some. Not Bonnie. Her parents died long ago—probably from the shock of seeing *her*. She's provided for by a trust. Marlene has a brother and sister living. They come and see her about once a month. I think they're trying to get the courts to give them control of her money before she gives it all away to the church. But Richard—"

"Can they do that?"

"What?"

"Get control of her money?"

"Well—it's not as easy as you might think. I know you hear stories about people being put away so that their relatives can get their money, but the courts protect people like Marlene these days."

He started to leave, and to keep him she said, "I'm afraid I don't know your name."

"Kirk. Kirk Tyner."

"Kirk, did you ever see any of *my* visitors?"

"No, I've only been here a short time. The doctor's other gardener retired."

Another patient went by, a fairly young one with a round head and bulging eyes which gave her the look of a pumpkin on a broomstick. "Great day," she shouted to the two of them. "Great day."

"Kirk," Gillian called from the kitchen, "I need raisins and flour. Can you drive into town for me?"

He picked up the handles of the wheelbarrow, but before leaving he asked Jane, "Is there anything I can get you from the village?"

It was a new concept, opening a whole line of possibilities. "Oh—let's see—" She stopped, wondering where she could get money. No one had mentioned the subject so far. "Well, not today. But some other time, thank you."

He lumbered off and she was alone again. Looking out at the rolling hills and sniffing the scented air, she wondered what was over the next rise. Evidently they were quite isolated, because she hadn't seen anyone yet who wasn't connected with the sanitarium. All kinds of emotions and desires churned within her. She wanted any number of nameless things. Some were connected with simply knowing what was over the hill as though she could hear distant pipes beckoning; others were related to experiences although she didn't know their nature; and the least of them were concerned with the need to consume either a food or a beverage she hadn't yet encountered here but had once been accustomed to. Before she could pluck the name of the latter from the spongy morass of her brain, she was distracted by a car motor. Instead of humming off into the distance, it turned up the sanitarium driveway. It couldn't be a visitor at this late hour. Besides, it wasn't even the weekend. Probably a late delivery truck.

But the car was a new black Cadillac. It stopped a short distance from her and a man got out, heading straight for her. She assumed he was lost and was going to ask for directions. He was slight and fair-haired, and a stranger, her subconscious told her, in the sense that he was not only someone she didn't know

now, but could never have known. He was extremely well
dressed, but the effect was unpleasant, at least to her. She couldn't
name the source of the unpleasantness. He wasn't even loudly
dressed, simply too perfectly dressed, as though expensive tailor-
ing was a new horizon in his life. The suit was dark blue and
faintly striped, the shirt light blue, the tie darkly patterned,
the shoes looked handmade, and there were all sorts of details
in the clothing which must have taken a long time to fashion.
She could also see the sparkle of a diamond ring on his finger.
He wasn't slight the way the doctor was slight (which was
healthy) but slight in a way that spoke of early deprivation.
His blond hair was a little too long and very smooth.

"Nice place," he said to Jane. "If you like the country, which
I don't happen to." His voice was the voice of the backwoods
or the mountains—she couldn't tell which.

"Uh, can I help you?" No longer anxious for company, she
felt unaccountably uneasy.

"Kind of ritzy too. Considerin' what it's for."

The word "ritzy" puzzled her, not because she didn't know
what it meant, but because the sanitarium hadn't struck her as
particularly ritzy.

"Three fifty a week if it's a cent," he went on. "Maybe more."

"Pardon me?" From what well of memory had she brought
up that cool, distant, "Pardon me?" putting an impassable barrier between them?

The man wasn't stupid. He glanced at her sharply. "Kind of
ritzy yourself, ain't you?" he drawled. "I mean for a body who
can't remember nothin'." He didn't look at her, but with elaborate casualness removed a cigarette case and lighter, each with a
diamond impaled in its gleaming gold surface, from his breast
pocket. He lit an expensive cigarette slowly and carefully and
blew out the smoke as though it were precious.

"Wh—what did you say? I mean about me not remembering
anything?"

He looked at her innocently. "Is that what I said?"

"How do *you* know I've lost my memory?"

"Oh, I don't know nothin'. I was only guessin'. I mean, you see a lady like you in a place like this"—he waved the cigarette —"and you know *somethin's* not right. You don't look like a nut, so I ask myself, what's a nice ladylike sickness, and I just naturally come to the conclusion that it's that thing where you lose your memory."

"Who are you?"

"Of course they's some—not you, ma'am—but some, who might be just pretendin' not to remember."

"Why should anyone do a thing like that?" Why wasn't she wheeling herself back to the house instead of prolonging this odd conversation?

He was examining the main house, the annex, the neighboring fields and the woods as though memorizing the setup. The garden didn't seem safe any longer, and the rise in the fields no longer beckoning. Turning, she saw no one but Beth, and she wondered if Gillian would be able to hear her if she had to scream.

"Yes, it sure is nice," he went on amiably. "Not for me, but nice for some. I mean, a lot nicer than other things I could mention."

"What kind of things?" she asked, knowing it was expected of her. She could see that he was picturing himself in the role of a cat playing with a mouse, and the fact reassured her a little. He was childish, and he wouldn't want the game to end too quickly. Of course, a childish mind in a grownup body could be dangerous.

"Oh, nicer than—fires, fer instance." He waited, but when she said nothing, he ventured a glance at her, but she kept her face wide-eyed and innocent. Disappointed, he said, "Nicer than accidents—"

"What kind of accidents?"

That pleased him. "All kinds of accidents. Like fallin' out of windows or drownin' or gettin' cut up—"

"Why did you come here?"

This question was out of order. Annoyed, he went through the elaborate pantomime of lighting a cigarette again. "What I'm sayin', ma'am, is you sure got it nice here. Nothin' to do but eat and sit around. Why spoil it?"

"What are you trying to tell me?" She felt it was important to know what his point was. He was so childish, he might wrap it up too well.

"*Me?* Tell *you* somethin', ma'am?" It was his turn to look wide-eyed. "I wouldn't tell a lady like you nothin'. I'm just makin' a comment. I said it's nice here, and if it was *me*, I'd keep it that way. I mean, why mess around with fancy doctors, like them what-do-you-call-'em, you know, the ones who make you remember things you have no business rememberin'?"

It was a switch, but this time *she* was supplying the word. "Psychiatrists?" she said slowly. With a sense of shock, she realized that she had been discussing psychiatrists only that afternoon with the doctor.

"Yeah, that's it. Why mess around? If I had it soft, I'd keep it that way. I'd play it dumb and go along for the ride."

"How did you know I was discussing a psychiatrist with Dr. Stires this afternoon?"

This was the best yet. He was pleased at her progress. He flicked an ash off his cuff, straightened his tie, shined his ring. "*Me* know what you and the doctor were discussin'? Not me, ma'am. I was just makin' conversation. The way I feel is, no one ought to go around askin' for trouble. They's some, they're better off without a memory. I'm not sayin' who. Just some. It's what you might call a—a—"

"An impersonal discussion?" she supplied again.

"That's right. You have a real nice way with words—for someone who can't remember."

"Who sent you here?"

"*Sent* me?" He sounded offended. "Nobody sends *me* anywheres, ma'am. I was passin' this here nice place and I like new places so I came up to look around. I like new places and I like to talk to people. Have them—you know—impersonal discussions. It's the only way to learn. Much better'n readin'. I never set any store by readin'. You get the wrong ideas that way. What I'm sayin' is, *big* people, *important* people, they're *doin'* things. The ones who can't *do* anythin'—they're the ones who are writin' books. So what's the good of the books?"

He stubbed out the second cigarette, rubbing it into the grass and seeming to enjoy the process. Was it that it gave him an opportunity to examine his shoes or that he enjoyed grinding an object into the ground? "Well, it's been real nice talkin' to you, but I got to be gettin' along." He didn't move, however. He felt, perhaps, that he had been too subtle, and that his message hadn't reached her. "You know, droppin' in places the way I do, I get to know lots of people. I mean, I got lots of friends—*everywhere.*" He glanced at her sharply.

"You mean you have friends *here?*"

"Well—" He hated to commit himself. "I'm not sayin' that, exactly. I mean, I have lots of friends, and I *could* have friends here." Finally satisfied that he'd created a work of art, he spun around and got back into his car. With a great grinding of gears, he shot down the driveway.

She listened to the sound of the motor until it was gone. As soon as the purr disappeared, she moved, as though released from a spell. It was as though he had never been, except that he had left an expensive scent behind, that and something else. But she had no word for it.

Instead came other words—"She left the web, she left the loom. She made three paces thro' the room. She saw the water lily bloom, she saw the helmet and the plume . . ."

What came after that? Something about the mirror cracking, and "'The curse is come upon me' cried the Lady of Shalott."

The curse is come upon me . . . Quickly she wheeled herself back to the safety of her own room, her own bed, her own shelf of nice, safe reading.

There was no doubt about what he had been telling her. She mustn't remember anything, and someone was watching her to make sure that she didn't.

6

Even while she was asleep, she had the sensation that the dream was familiar and that she had gone through it many times before. It began with fuzzy, annoying incidents—a gray street, a store window with nothing in it but drapery, unknown faces, unrecognized voices and then a woman saying: "If only children would listen! How much pain they could spare themselves!"

"Everyone has to learn by experience, you know." That was her own voice.

"Remember that line from *Tess of the D'Urbervilles*? About 'experience making one unfit for further travel'? Sometimes—"

"Oh God, Mother! The way not to have experiences is to be dead."

Someone was laughing. It was a pleasant, high-pitched laugh and the room had changed. "Try a watercress sandwich." This was another woman, but motherly too. Someone she knew very well . . .

"Don't you start on me too." Her own voice again, faintly accusing.

"Listen, honey, you're awfully young—"

"Everyone harps on my age. It's a disease that corrects itself. And how old were *you* when you got married?"

"That was different. My family knew his for years."

"I bet Mother told you to talk to me. Listen, no one who's ever been in love—if you'll pardon the expression—listens to someone else's advice. If they do, they're not in love."

"At least don't rush into it. I've heard stories about him. Very unpleasant ones."

"I don't want to hear them."

"You've got to hear them. You'll ruin your life if you marry him . . ."

The room faded. It had been sunny, and the sensations surrounding it had all been pleasant, but now she was somewhere else and she was frightened. She was walking, hurrying down a dark street, but it wasn't the darkness that made her anxious, but apprehension about her errand. It made her stomach churn the way it had when she'd been at boarding school and had had to get up to make a speech in class.

She was standing outside a door and the dread was thick and hot like steam all around her. Why was it still dark? There had been lights in the hall—no, she was in a small vestibule and the only light came from a crack under the door to the sitting room. What was she doing here? Suppose someone came out and asked her? If they ever found her listening in the dark, what would they do?

Their voices were soft and it was hard to hear what they were saying. But she had to know. It was connected with something important. Most of the time they spoke so softly she could only hear the low, indistinguishable hum, but now and then someone got excited and whole phrases were audible.

"—a fortune to him. Don't go higher than three thousand—" It belonged to an unknown person. What would happen if she pushed the door a fraction of an inch? Would it creak? She pushed but it didn't give.

"He must know they'll get him. What makes you sure he'll go through with it?" She recognized that voice. She knew it better than her own.

A silence. Sounds she couldn't interpret. Then, "—plead insanity. He wants to get his family out. He'll do it all right. Besides, we've made other arrangements . . ."

She couldn't hear the question that followed, but she heard a laugh. Then a chair moved. Panic welled up in her chest. She was running again, running through the swirling blackness. It seemed to her that she was being followed—no, it was only a drunk who had been sitting on the curb and had started up after her . . .

She sat up in bed, her chest a cage with a crazed animal pounding to get out. She felt as if she were choking. What had happened to terrify her like this? Something awful had taken place—no, it was *about* to take place and only she could stop it. But what was it? If only she could remember, she could prevent an appalling catastrophe.

But it was a dream. She had had a nightmare, and somehow she had convinced herself that she was in a unique position to stop a calamity. What had awakened her? Fear or—no, it was a sound in the hall. Where in the world was she?

Gradually the room came into focus. The night table, the chair, the vase.

She was in the sanitarium, Dr. Stires's sanitarium, and there was nothing to be afraid of. Outside her window she could see the thickened branches of the trees, pregnant with buds, and the oyster luminescence of the moon, half shielding, half revealing the landscape as though it were under a shell. If she could pry it open, she could see the mystery within.

That sound in the hall again. Probably the dog—what was his name? Hopeless? Helpless?

If she didn't allow herself to be constantly distracted by extraneous noises, perhaps she could remember the dream. She couldn't get over the idea that it was vital to recall the thing that hadn't happened yet. She lay back again, and the moment her head touched the pillow the aura of evil returned. It was agonizingly close.

Then she lost it completely as she heard a cry from the hallway. She was up like a spring, her legs dangling over the side of the bed. Dizziness overcame her and she steadied herself by holding on to the table. "Zee!"

The sounds from the hall became rhythmic, odd smacking thuds as though someone were hitting the wall. They didn't seem threatening, but the fact that they were inexplicable was enough to frighten her. "Zee! Gillian! Zee!"

Zee's bedsprings groaned, a light switch clicked, and then, wearing only a nightgown, Zee stood in the doorway, rubbing her eyes and shivering a little. "Wh—what's the matter?"

"The hall—quick—there's something there—no, wait, be careful—oh if I could only walk—"

Switching on the light in Jane's room, Zee hesitated, and then, very carefully, she opened the door to the hall. Evidently there was no danger, because she slammed back the door and stepped out.

At first Jane couldn't relate what was happening to anything in her experience. A creature in a robe was bunched up like a foetus on the floor just outside the room, and then, abruptly, the limbs spread-eagled in a spasmodic convulsion. Again and again the thing contracted and expanded, the head arching back, the eyes open, saliva spilling from the mouth. A pool was spreading around the lower body. Both head and heels banged the floor in the repulsive rhythm.

Both women stared, transfixed, but just then Gillian's daughter, Adeline, who slept in the annex, came running down the hallway and dropped on her knees. She had a padded tongue depressor which she quickly inserted in the open mouth. There was a gurgling, rattling breath, and at the same moment the convulsions ceased. The thing on the floor stopped its fantastic gyrations and Jane recognized Beth, the one with the brother.

Zee and Adeline lifted her off the floor and carried her down the hall. In a moment Zee reappeared, looking shaken. "I never saw a fit before. It's scary, isn't it?"

Jane took a deep breath and shut her eyes, as exhausted as if it had been she instead of Beth who had had the convulsions. Did injuries of the kind she had sustained ever lead to fits, she wondered. Suppose *she* ever looked like that?

Zee patted her pillow and turned off the light. Before she left, however, Jane asked her, "Aren't you rather a heavy sleeper for a nurse?"

"Me?" Zee asked defensively. "I hear *you* whenever you need anything. People are always tuned in on their own responsibilities. It's like a mother. She can hear her own baby cry even if it's on the other side of the house."

"Is that true?" Jane asked with interest. "Oh—well, good night."

When Zee left, she couldn't sleep. She watched the trees outside, considering their metamorphosis at night. During the day they seemed to be decorative models, waiting to be painted, but at night they become spies, watching her every movement.

Now *there* was a sick thought. How did she know she wasn't as unbalanced as the others? She kept assuming that she was different, but wasn't she as much a monstrosity in her own way as Beth? *Her* convulsions happened to be hidden.

Her thoughts whirled on and on, occasionally so depressing she felt she couldn't bear them, other times simply annoying. Images and voices from another existence shot past her inner eye so quickly she couldn't discern their meaning. Then, just before she fell asleep, she was conscious of the same aura of evil she had felt before and another phrase slithered through her mind—"One thing's for sure—he'll get it no matter who has to pull the trigger . . ."

7

"What did he look like?" the doctor asked. His voice held an odd note in it, one she hadn't heard before and couldn't identify.

"He was small, you know, slender and he had light hair and I suppose you could call him good-looking in a way. He had his hair slicked down with a lot of uh—"

"Hair dressing?"

"Yes. He was very—how can I explain it—expensively dressed, but not well dressed. You could tell he wasn't uh—"

"A gentleman?" He smiled faintly.

"Right." She smiled too. "And he spoke with an accent. He—"

"You mean he was foreign?"

"No. He was from another part of the country—I'm not sure which."

"Then what happened?"

"He seemed threatening, and yet I'm not sure he actually said anything you could call a threat. He hinted I would be better off if I didn't get my memory back."

"How better off?"

She started to answer but her attention was momentarily distracted by Marlene, the aristocratic one. Elaborately dressed, even to the point of wearing a hat, she went past carrying a sack of birdseed. She stopped at the outer edge of the lawn and began filling the birdhouse.

"She looks so—so normal," Jane said abruptly.

"Yes." Silence filled the space between them like a heavy gas. Jane looked normal too. Then, "Go on," he said.

"Well, he implied that there were spies watching me."

"Spies!" the doctor exploded.

"That's what he said. And it must be true because he mentioned the fact that we had spoken about getting a psychiatrist earlier the same day. How would he know that?"

"What are the spies supposed to be for?" His face was blank.

"To make sure I didn't remember anything."

"How could they do that?"

"I mean to make sure that if I *did* remember anything, I wouldn't tell anyone about it."

"Remember what?"

"Are you being stupid on purpose?" she asked, losing her patience for the first time that she could remember. "Naturally I don't know."

The doctor lit a cigarette and smoked for a while, keeping his face slightly averted. Finally, conscious of the passage of time and the fact that she could get only a limited amount of his allotted hour or two, she said, "You told me we'd talk about me today. That you'd tell me more."

"What do you want to know?"

"Everything. That is, I *think* I want to know everything. I don't even know how old I am."

"You're nearly twenty-three. You went to a junior college. Let's see, I don't know many girls' schools—Bradford, I think. Does that ring a bell?"

She shook her head.

His voice droned on, intermingling with the pleasant clatter of china as the cook prepared dinner. It was the kind of still day which carried every sound and she could hear the distant mooing of cows. The air was redolent with scents which seeped under the doors of her closed mind, invading hidden corners and filling her with tantalizing glimpses of past delights or, perhaps, future ones. "Your father died long ago—a kidney infection, I think." The words had no connection with her sensations. They were completely outside. "Your family has a great deal of money, so there was no financial hardship involved. Let's see—your mother never remarried and the two of you were very close, I believe. You went to various exclusive schools"—she could detect a faintly derisive note in his voice—"before college, and afterwards you did settlement work with young children. You lived in a town house in the East Seventies, I think, and in the summers you either went to Europe or lived in Newport. There's also a farm in the South—or there was. Everything was sold after your mother died because, well, no one knew when you'd be able to use them."

"How did my mother die?"

He puffed a moment. "She had a heart attack."

"When?"

"Not too long ago."

"You mean it was brought on by what happened to me?"

Cautiously he said, "I believe she had had a heart condition for some time."

"But my accident probably killed her." The words meant nothing. She frowned faintly, trying to hold on to a memory. It was connected with a dream, but again she was distracted. The patient who was always smiling, Richard, ambled over to the doctor and picked up the newspapers at the latter's feet. He stared at them intently, as though reading.

"And my trustee takes care of everything?"

"Yes. He was the one who authorized—who made all the decisions."

"You started to say something. Authorized what?"

"What was needed."

"When may I see the friends you spoke about?"

"Any time. I have the names and addresses of everyone who called."

Richard gave up the newspapers and began digging with his hands in the garden. Kirk, passing with cans of paint, told him to stop messing up the grounds. A thought occurred to her. "Did any of the people who called sound like the man I described?"

"You mean as though they had an accent?"

"Yes. Or, well—uneducated."

"On the contrary, they sounded very well educated."

"And that's all I have? A trustee and some friends?"

"Don't downrate it. Did I ever tell you the story of the man who wanted to find out how many friends he had and he—"

"You didn't answer me. Is that all I have?"

"Not exactly."

Impatiently she said, "I never saw anyone as evasive as you are. You're always holding something back. For instance, when I was telling you about this man who spoke to me yesterday, I sensed something uh—served?"

"Reserved."

"Yes. Reserved about your attitude. Now you're acting that way again. What do you mean by 'not exactly'?"

"Well, there's the man who was your escort that night. The one who took you to the theater."

"The theater?"

"Where you had the accident."

"It happened in a theater? How?"

He took a deep breath. "I've told you."

"I'm sorry. I have this feeling you've told me and then—it's awful, I know, but I can't seem to separate what happened from what I dreamed. I'm never sure. But I *am* getting better all the time, am I not?"

"Yes, of course. There was a fire."

"Oh." There was a sense of recognition without a definite memory and she didn't want him to continue. She tried to head him off. "Where *is* that mooing coming from? Is there a farm nearby?"

He stared at her a moment. "You were burned pretty badly."

She wanted to continue chatting about the cow, but the way he had behaved before made her hesitate. His manner toward her had been doubtful and she didn't want him to think that her mind was wandering. Brightly she asked, "And that's what caused my amnesia?"

"No. It was the fall. You were on a mezzanine and it collapsed."

There it was again, seeping under the closed doors of her mind, the noxious poison of fear. And with it came a sound, the sound of— She started to put her hands up to her ears, but she checked the movement in time. Quickly she said, "Tell me about my escort."

He was watching her closely, but his voice was neutral. "He was, is, rather, your fiancé."

"My fiancé!" She had found an effective barrier at last. The revelation obliterated everything else. "What's he like? Has he been here? Tell me all about him. I knew you were keeping something back."

"Yes, he's been here, but you weren't quite— He calls at least once a week."

"Then he knows that I'm normal? I mean—almost normal?"
"Yes."
"When may I see him?"
"Any time you like."

"Right away—tomorrow. That is"—she glanced down at herself—"I ought—I don't even have makeup—" Her eyes came to rest on her left hand. "Why don't I have an engagement ring?"

"I don't know. You weren't wearing one when you came here. Perhaps you'd better speak to him about it. His name is Austin Berquist, by the way."

The absence of the ring bothered her. Another oddity. Nothing was clear cut—everything shaded off into unknown territory. "What does he look like?"

"Oh. You'll approve." The faintly derisive note again.

"Do you have a picture?"

"As far as I know there wasn't one in your trunks. When your mother died, the housekeeper packed your belongings. I suppose the pictures went into storage with the rest."

"Never mind. What is he like? I mean his character—his work—"

"I can't vouch for his character, but he seems pleasant. He's a lawyer. He went to Williams or Brown—one of those."

She tried to evoke a picture, but nothing at all happened, not the faintest essence of anything. It was like a painting. One could have the ingredients—canvas, brushes, paint—but that didn't mean one could create a work of art.

Kirk and Richard were back again and Richard went to the swing and began pumping. There was something terrible about the sight of a grown man dangling on the child's toy. Beth, apparently unaffected by her experience of the night before, appeared and watched him.

"I would like to buy some things before my uh—before Austin comes. May I send Kirk to the village? Do I have any money?"

"You may charge what you like, but don't uh—well don't give him too much responsibility. He's not really sick but—"

"You mean— But I thought— Is Kirk a patient too?"

He nodded.

"I thought he worked here."

"He does—it helps pay for his keep. But he's an epileptic. Of course he's fine most of the time, but—well, I want you to understand that most epileptics can lead normal, self-supporting lives. But Kirk is apparently one of those unfortunates whose seizures don't yield to treatment. His mother told me that they've tried everything and the doctors decided he needed institutional care."

Nothing was the way it seemed. The world was filled with people who had something convulsing within them. Even a nice, normal-appearing gardener like Kirk. Or Marlene. And then, why not the doctor? Or Gillian or Zee? If there was no outer way to judge—

"Why was your voice so odd when I told you about the man who spoke to me yesterday?" she asked.

"I wasn't aware of the fact that it was odd."

"Yes, it was. As though—as though—"

"Yes?"

"As though you doubted my word."

He was silent, and the sense of shock went through her, the same sort of shock she had had when she had realized that Zee was borrowing her clothing. They had discounted her—in one case, her right to ownership, in the other, her right to be believed.

Tearing up bits of newspaper and allowing them to drop on the lawn, she said, "I want to see my fiancé as soon as possible."

"All right," he said mildly, and stood up, sensing that she had dismissed him. "I'll call him."

As he walked away, she was overcome by depression. She had considered the amnesia temporary, akin to a morning mist which would clear away as the sun became stronger. But suppose it was only a symptom of a much greater damage to her brain which, by the nature of the damage itself, she could never sense. Suppose it was a degeneration that could produce hallucinations and imaginary conversations and a whole nonexistent world. All of it—the hints of wealth, the fiancé, the hospital itself—could be concoctions of her own brain.

8

All morning she'd felt as though a dentist drill were working into her nerves. She was waiting for Austin.

One glimpse of his face could possibly bring it all back and then she would be whole again, but the thought gave her no comfort. It wouldn't be like a spotlight, illuminating one area only. It might show her everything, including the thing she wasn't supposed to remember.

She was outdoors in the wheel chair, watching the driveway. She had become quite familiar with the untenanted gatehouse on the other side of the road. Beside her, the transistor radio on the garden table blared about discoveries in space, deaths in Asia, civil rights riots and then, ". . . since the governor's assassination, a new law . . ."

What nerve was struck there? Which governor? The only assassinated governor she had ever heard about had been Huey Long—no, he had been a senator at the time. And anyway, why bring it up now? She had to find out more about recent history. There was so much to do, so much to learn and all she did was sit in chairs watching the world—

"Would you like me to wheel you down to the birdhouse, Miss Wallcutt?" It was Marlene, the aristocratic one. "You can see wonderful specimens this time of the year. Yesterday we were visited by a red-winged blackbird and two cardinals. I think I also saw a Baltimore oriole. The coloring was right, but he was too quick for me."

Touched, Jane said, "I would love to, thank you, but I'll have to do it another time. I'm expecting a visitor."

Always the soul of discretion, Marlene inclined her head and went on her way. Gillian came out for air, saw Jane and strolled over. "Today is the big day, isn't it?" she asked jovially.

"Well, I don't know how big it will be, but it's the day all right." She covered her cheeks with the palms of her hands. "Do you have a mirror with you?"

"You look fine. Truthfully, you've changed so much since you first came here, I hardly recognize you. I'm proud of you."

Just then a small foreign car came up the driveway and Jane felt faint. "Don't go," she begged Gillian, but Gillian, having none of Marlene's discretion, had no intention of moving. They both stared as the car stopped in front of the semicircle at the door. From it came a tallish, well-coordinated-looking man. He walked toward Jane without a moment's hesitation. She was flooded with emotions, but it was hard to isolate the individual components. She couldn't see his features immediately, but he walked well, with long, easy strides. He was like a picture coming slowly into focus. First she saw the brown hair, then the narrow face, and finally the remote, completely expressionless eyes.

At that moment she had a reaction she was completely unprepared for. She had counted on embarrassment perhaps, or with luck, some flicker of recognition, but what happened was totally unexpected. She was conscious of intense fear. No sense of recognition, only terror.

She wet her lips and tried to mutter something, but her voice cracked. She was behaving like a fool, she thought furiously, conscious of her hot cheeks and quivering chin. Like a nonqualified applicant for a job, or worse still, like a schoolgirl at her first party. It was Gillian who was carrying the ball, providing the chitchat to get them past their first few minutes. Wagging a flirtatious finger at him, she was saying, "What took you so long? This poor girl has been waiting all day for you." The blood rushing to her head made it impossible for her to hear his response, but his voice sounded deep and pleasant. Unable to look at him, she did a number of idiotic things like change the radio station and stare intently at a passing car. While she fiddled, he got chairs and the two of them settled down. "Does she seem different to you?" Gillian was asking. The question stopped her activity for a moment as she waited for an answer. It seemed to be a long time in coming. Finally he said, "Well, not really. Just as though she'd gone through a lot."

They went on discussing her as though she weren't present, but although his remarks were addressed to Gillian, she knew with an instinct that went deeper than memory that his attention was on her. It had a quality in it that was new to her remembered experience and she had no name for it. It gave her a heightened awareness and a stimulation, a sense of excitement that nearly drowned the fear.

"Did you recognize me at all?"

She jumped visibly when she realized he had spoken to her directly. She much preferred having him talk to Gillian. Trying not to act like an idiot, she stammered, "No—I can't—I had no resation whatsoever."

She caught a sideways glimpse of his frown and realized she had made a mistake. Miserably, like a half-tame bird, darting forward for a crumb and hopping away at the slightest movement, she said, "I get the words mixed up—uh—the doctor said, he said it won't last." God, I sound like an idiot, she thought. To make up for it, she said brightly, "How was your trip up? I hope it didn't take too long. Do you live far from here?" She saw that she was making it worse. He would probably never come again, she thought desperately and wondered at her deep sensation of desolation at the thought. And yet the dread was still there. He began talking to Gillian again and her apprehension died down. She caught phrases now and then—

"We were just about last, and the band struck up just as we entered—"

She wondered what he was talking about, but it didn't really matter much. She wanted him to continue endlessly, stay close by and yet not make any demands upon her. Darting glances at him when she was sure his attention was on Gillian, she saw that he was a little older than she had thought at first, but at the same time, almost too handsome. She remembered the doctor's derisive, "Oh, you'll approve." Uneasily she wondered what he thought of her. She had gotten Zee to wash her hair and set it, and she had a suntan, but she felt her clothes weren't right. They had been bought some time before the accident and no longer fit her thinned-down figure. In addition, the styles had apparently changed because the skirt was too long. She felt dowdy and unsure of herself.

"She could never stay still," he was telling Gillian, and she realized they were discussing herself. "She was always afraid life was passing her by and once she called me and said, 'Let's have dinner in Bermuda.' She wanted to charter a plane, have dinner and come back the same evening."

Without thinking, she asked, "Did we do it?"

He turned his eyes on her and the fear and confusion swelled back visibly into her face. "No," he said. "I told you you were an ass."

Gillian laughed. "Now that's a nice thing for a boy to tell his intended."

His eyes rested on Jane a moment longer and then he went on with his recital. Gillian's use of the word "intended" had been the first mention of any relationship between them and she wanted to study his expression but she was afraid he might look at her again.

"—terrible student in school. Stayed in by the skin of her teeth."

She wondered at his tactlessness. If their positions had been reversed she would never have spoken that way.

"—never saw anyone so generous with money, but when it came to her own comfort—well, she'd forget other people's feelings. She'd be late for appointments, snub people she'd been with the night before. It wasn't that she was really selfish, only thoughtless—"

His eyes flicked over her and she began pushing down the

cuticle on her nails. She wanted to defend herself, but she had
no tools for doing so. She couldn't refute any of it.

"She was a great athlete—" He stopped, as though noticing for
the first time that he was being tactless, and she thought it was
odd that he felt embarrassed about discussing something which
hardly interested her at all, and yet completely indifferent about
reporting personality failures which troubled her so much more.

"Oh, she'll walk again," Gillian assured him. "Go on. I like
hearing all about Jane. She couldn't tell us anything."

"Well," he went on, almost absent-mindedly, as though his
mind was on something else, "she could do about anything she
made up her mind to do. She could have been so many things
but all she wanted to do was play tennis or golf, or ski or—at the
—that is, before the—she was even talking about taking up para-
chute jumping. She would get bored—we used to argue about
it—" His voice trailed off and to keep him talking, Gillian asked,
"Did you argue a lot?"

"What? Oh—well, probably not more than most engaged
couples."

A nerve vibrated. He had brought it up himself. Engaged.
Suddenly she wished Gillian would leave them alone. It wasn't
that she was no longer afraid, but that the other thing was
stronger. She didn't need Gillian anymore.

"—volunteer work for a settlement house. The children absolutely adored her. She was like the pied piper, but she'd get
restless—"

"She was young," Gillian said soothingly. "She needed set-
tling down."

"I got settled all right," she said suddenly and was appalled at
her own words, but they weren't paying any attention because
Gillian was asking, "What did she look like before the accident?"

Even he seemed taken aback. "Oh—about what she looks like
now."

"Pretty?" Gillian asked avidly.

"She still is."

"Of course she is. I mean—it can't be the same, can it? Do you have a picture?"

He hesitated and glanced at Jane, but she continued to stare at her own hands. Finally, reluctantly, he took a wallet from his breast pocket and began poking around the assortment of cards. When he found what he was looking for—a worn-out, dog-eared picture—he glanced at it and a shadow crossed his face. A truck lumbered by on the road and Jane turned to stare at it woodenly as Gillian reached for the picture.

"Oh, she's beautiful," Gillian breathed. "Here, Jane, look at it."

For a moment she behaved as though she hadn't heard and then she accepted the square of cardboard. She glanced at him quickly and then shied away from the intensity of his expression.

It wasn't a snapshot. It was a small version of a studio portrait. She looked at it sadly for a long time. It was herself, but with a sparkle, a gaiety, something indefinable that no longer existed. Eve before the fall. Silently she returned the picture to him, and when his fingers brushed hers, she shied from that also.

"Are you afraid of something?" he asked abruptly.

Instantly it washed over her like a wave, and like a wave it made her feel as though she were choking. She knew where the fear stemmed from. "Austin," she said sharply, using his name for the first time, "why did my family try to talk me out of marrying you?"

Nothing could have been more devoid of expression than his face. It was completely blank. He glanced at Gillian, but she was far too fascinated to take the hint.

"What did you say?" he asked Jane slowly.

"My mother warned me not to marry you."

"How could you remember a thing like that?"

She felt bewildered. She put her hand to her forehead and was afraid she was going to black out. Something tenuous, vague, more like a vapor than anything tangible, was tantalizing her with its nearness and its elusiveness. "I don't know—I—maybe I dreamed—" Her heart was pumping frantically and she couldn't go on. "It was nothing," she finished breathlessly. "Just a dream."

He remained a moment longer, his eyes, she felt, boring into her head seeing memories even she couldn't find. Finally, after another glance at Gillian, he rose. "The doctor told me not to stay too long the first time."

All the excitement drained out of her, and the disappointment was worse than anything that had gone before. With a tremendous sense of lost opportunity she looked at Gillian and wondered what would have happened if she hadn't asked her to stay. She remained in the chair watching the road long after his car disappeared.

9

On the palm of the doctor's hand was a small coin with oriental letters around a square hole in the center. He held it out for her inspection, watching her face.

She felt dizzy again, but instead of lowering her head, she lifted it, as though seeking help from the long vistas, the pale, shredded clouds in the distance. It was the wrong thing to do.

"What's the matter?" he asked sharply. "What happened?"

As she put her hand out for the coin, she almost slipped from the wheel chair, and he grabbed her and pushed her head down into her lap. After a moment she said, "Let me up. I'm all right." Gently he helped her back and watched her face. "Well? Obviously the coin means something to you."

She reached out again and he put it into her hand. Turning it slowly, she asked, "Where did you get it?"

"It was in your hand when they—when you were found."

"What is it?"

"What is it? Oh, you mean—well, it's a five-chu piece, they tell me, copper, and quite old. About 500 A.D. And it's Chinese. Does it mean anything to you?"

"I—I wanted to die when I saw it."

Eagerly he said, "Then you remember it!"

"No—that is, I don't know. It just makes me feel terrible. I don't want to think about it." She shut her eyes, as though to blot out a vision. Then, without realizing what she was doing, she began to rub her legs. She was lying in a protected area between the annex and the toolhouse in a swim suit and she could see the marks of the grafts on her legs.

"You're the most inconsistent person I ever met," he said in exasperation. "One minute you're all for getting better—asking about physical therapists and psychiatrists—and the next, you shut your mind again." Pointing to Bonnie, who was nodding and jabbering, he added, "Perhaps you'd be better off like that." Bonnie offered Jane a scrap of paper, and when Jane shook her head, the dwarf ambled off to give it to Kirk, who was painting the toolshed. He too refused and she went to find Marlene.

"What an awful thing to say," Jane whispered in a barely audible voice. She had hesitated before speaking, afraid she would burst into tears.

"We've asked your fiancé and your trustee about the coin, but neither one of them had the slightest idea where you'd gotten it."

She said nothing, and after a moment he continued: "I thought at first that you'd pulled it off someone in the confusion, but now that I've seen your reaction to it—"

"I don't want to talk about it," she said in a voice that was nearly a shout. It ripped through the quiet, making Gillian's daughter, Adeline, look out of the window, stopping the ever-smiling Richard on his way to nowhere, and even causing the birds to flutter from the lawn to the trees. "I'm sorry," she said.

He dropped the coin in his trouser pocket.

"It's like having a nightmare," she went on. "You wake up and you don't remember it. You only have the sensation of fright. And then, when you put your head on the pillow again, you get a flash of it, not really a memory, but just the fear again."

"I understand," he agreed, nodding. "But if you want to be healthy again, you'll have to take the bad part with the good. Amnesia is often selective. Certain things are remembered and others forgotten, not necessarily for physical reasons."

"What governor was killed recently?"

He stared at her a moment and then finally sighed. "All right. We won't discuss the coin."

"No—really. I want to know. I seem to get a definite reaction when I hear it mentioned."

"Paynter. Governor Paynter. He was campaigning for his second term as governor, and it happened as he got off the plane in—" In the midst of lighting a cigarette, the doctor absent-mindedly flicked out the match. "You know something? It happened the day of the fire."

They both considered that for a moment and then he went on. "A South American shot him—a crackpot—and he, in turn, was killed by one of the state policemen."

"Why did he do it?"

"Why did who do what?"

"The assassin—why did he kill the governor?"

"Oh—" He smiled. "You know those South Americans. Very emotional. If he had a reason, no one knows it. There was all kinds of talk."

"What kind?"

"Oh—that he was offered money to bring his family to the United States if he did it—"

"Who offered him money? Who were the governor's enemies?"

"Don't get so worked up about it. It was just talk. Some people see plots everywhere. In the end, everyone agreed that the man was simply unbalanced." He finally lit the cigarette and stood up. "I'm expecting a patient in my office soon. I'll see you tomorrow." He walked away, stopping to chat with people as usual, and heading for the kitchen to give Gillian some instructions. She watched him a moment and then she shut her eyes. She was beginning to feel chilly. It wasn't suntanning weather yet, but she had talked Zee into allowing her to do it. Zee, as usual, had gone inside to chat with the help. After a while, she sat up, deciding it was time to change for dinner. Just as she moved, she saw something glinting far off in the woods. Leaning forward, she tried to see what it was, but the distance was fuzzy. There was no doubt, as the doctor had told her about her vocal chords, that her eyes must have been injured too. She pushed the wheel chair forward, and at that moment she heard a sharp crack, as though a branch had snapped, from the direction of the woods. At the same moment a splinter of wood flew off the tree to the left of and just behind her.

Still more surprised than alarmed, she leaned forward to peer at the ground. Just below the nick in the tree was a piece of dark gray lead. She had no specific knowledge of guns or bullets, but she knew immediately what it was. She picked it up, turned as she heard a sound behind her, and found Bonnie at her elbow. Before Jane could guess at her intention, Bonnie grabbed the bullet.

"Give it to me," Jane snapped, but Bonnie grunted and tottered off.

"Wait—stop." Jane turned the wheel chair and started after her. "Bonnie!" she shouted. "Come back."

Poking her head out of one of the windows, Gillian called, "What's the matter?"

"Gillian! Come here. I've been shot at!"

"What?" In a moment Gillian came flying out of the house, wiping her hands on her apron. "What did you say?"

"I've been shot at. Bonnie took the bullet. Get it from her."

"Honestly, Jane, if anyone heard you—"

"Hurry! Go after Bonnie." Bonnie had disappeared around the side of the house, and as she spoke, Jane tried to manipulate the wheel chair.

"Truthfully, you talk so foolish. And sitting out here half naked when it isn't even—"

"Will you please go after Bonnie?" Jane shouted.

"All right. Stop yelling. You'll upset the others. Do you want me to call the doctor? He just—"

"*Get Bonnie.*"

Gillian went off in the direction taken by Bonnie, and Jane tried to follow, but the ground was too uneven for the wheels. Several patients had turned up and were watching with interest, but none offered to help. Finally Gillian returned. "She didn't have anything but her usual junk."

"Are you sure?"

"Of course I'm sure."

"Then she must have dropped it. We'll have to search the ground—"

"If you think I have time to search the ground now—well, I don't. I have to help with dinner. Anyway you dreamed it. Who would be shooting here?"

Suddenly Jane had a thought. "Come here."

Gillian stared at her but didn't move.

"I said come here. I want to show you something."

"What do you want to show me?"

Jane stared at her, and gradually the dull red color came into her cheeks again. Gillian was afraid of her. She wanted to shout at her, tell her what a fool she was, but she knew enough to take a deep breath and wait for her temper to cool. When she was sure she could control her voice, she said quietly, "I want to show you the spot where the bullet nicked the tree."

"Where?"

Jane pointed. "There. On the oak."

"How do you know it's an oak?"

Jane stared at her incredulously. Taking a deep breath, she said slowly and distinctly, "Because I've seen acorns under it."

Gillian wasn't stupid. This time *she* flushed. She went to the tree, but kept Jane in sight. By this time they had been joined by Zee and Beth, and Gillian was more confident. She peered at the tree. "There's a mark there. It could have happened any time."

"It's fresh," Jane said in the same careful voice, and explained to Zee what had happened.

"Bonnie or Richard could have done it," Gillian suggested.

"I think it was a hunter," said Zee. "Once I was in the woods with Gib when he came to visit me on a case with an old woman who had a stroke, and we heard this shot and suddenly some pebbles behind Gib—"

"My brother give me pebbles," Beth contributed. "Very pretty. You come my room and I show you."

"Well, I can't stand here all day," Gillian said. "I have to take care of twenty people."

Nonetheless, the three of them continued the discussion, and quietly Jane wheeled herself back to the annex. She wasn't sure which thought was uppermost—that her life depended upon her getting away from this madhouse, or that she was as mad as the rest of them and had imagined the entire incident.

10

Someone was calling her. The voice, achingly familiar, came from a remote, inaccessible point of time. It reached out from a far-off region that, in some mysterious fashion, was no longer within her grasp.

She stirred, groaned, and finally opened her eyes. Moonlight touched the vase, turning it into a prism of sparks. Outside, the trees were motionless, waiting, like herself, for something to happen. From the distance came the baying of a pack of dogs. In a few minutes a wild creature would be torn to pieces.

Who was calling?

Her head was like a cavity filled with cotton wool. And the bed felt as though she were the princess who could sense the presence of a pea under twenty mattresses. Then she heard something incredible—the faint tinkle of a music box behind her. She started to sit up, but fell back again, the room whirling dangerously. "Jane, Jane," a voice called from that place beyond time.

Was she dreaming? What an odd assortment of dreams she was having lately. She would never be able to untangle the real from the unreal. Had someone really shot at her this afternoon?

"Zee!" She waited, but nothing happened. "Zee!"

No response. Evidently the nurse had gone to the main house either for a snack or in order to watch the late show with Gillian. Adeline was probably with them, too. Which left herself and poor staggering, epileptic Beth.

Her uneasiness increased, and with it came a childish sense of abandonment. All the grownups had left, and no matter how much she cried, no one would come to her.

There was something about that tune . . .

But she could remember neither the melody nor what there was about it that made her afraid. Her breathing was shallow and took a great deal of effort. It was like the time they had put an object she couldn't see over her mouth and nose and everything had blended together—the lights and the faces, the white walls—

"Jane, Jane, do you hear me, Jane?"

She tried to sit up again but felt too weak. The whole thing was impossible. No one was calling. It was just that her battered brain had gotten its signals mixed and produced an auditory hallucination. Then came the faint sound of the music box again, so soft it was almost nothing more than a rustling, a whisper.

"Tannenbaum." How odd. In March. She had always known it. Ever since—ever since what? Her mother's voice telling her, "Of course we'll sing 'Tannenbaum.' You've behaved peculiarly about that song ever since you were four and—"

A blank. What happened when she was four to make her afraid of a song? At the time she had known what her mother had been referring to, but now—

The music box purled into muffled sound again.

> O Tannenbaum, O Tannenbaum,
> You are the tree most loved!
> How oft you've given me delight
> When Christmas fires were burning bright . . .

Now she had it. "Ever since you were four and Vista was burned."

Her little cat, Vista. They had been playing "Tannenbaum" indoors, and outdoors they had started a bonfire. No one had seen the cat under the pile of brush until that terrible cry—

"Jane, Jane, listen, Jane."

Where was the voice coming from? Behind the bed or outside the door or from her own head?

"Don't remember anything, Jane. Don't try to remember what happened before the accident, Jane. If you remember, it will be much worse than anything, Jane. Worse than the fire—"

The voice was familiar. She knew it better than her own. The liquids of her stomach were curdling, turning sour and making her want to throw up. And she couldn't move. It was as though she were encased in an envelope of cobwebs.

"If you remember, Jane, something terrible will happen to you. We'll get you, Jane. We'll get you tomorrow or next week or next year and it won't be easy, Jane. It will be worse than the fire . . ."

In a moment she would know where she had heard that voice before. If it continued talking, the revelation would explode within her head, illuminating every corner, but then the music box opened again.

> . . . *your faithful leaves will teach me*
> *That hope and love and constancy*
> *Give joy and peace eternally . . .*

"Don't tell anyone about tonight, Jane. We'll be watching you. If you tell anyone—"

The silence was so abrupt it was like the click of a switch. For a moment she heard nothing but the crickets. Then footsteps sounded outside her door and Zee's white uniform appeared, ghostly in the moonlight. "What was that?" she asked sharply.

Jane's head whirled in confusion. Blurrily she asked, "Did you hear it too?"

"Of course I heard it. Somebody whispering."

Waves of relief washed over her. It wasn't something she had imagined. She reached out and grasped Zee's hand. "I'm so glad you're here. I called you—"

"You were asleep so I went out to watch television. What were you doing? Did you have the radio on?"

"No, it wasn't the radio. Feel it. It's cool."

"I don't have to feel it. I believe you. Besides, I heard someone say Jane. Who was it?"

"I don't know. I woke up and I heard this voice saying, 'Jane,

Jane,' and then a music box started up. The voice told me something terrible would happen to me if I remembered anything from the past. It also said not to tell anyone about tonight—"

"But that's crazy. It doesn't make sense." Zee's voice dropped to a whisper and she glanced around fearfully. She didn't put on the light, but drew the curtain over the French doors.

"I know it's crazy. That's why I'm glad you heard it too."

"Who would do a thing like that?"

"You'll have to telephone the doctor. Go to the main house and—"

"Now?"

"Yes, now. We can't wait."

"But the doctor'll be asleep. Besides—"

"He won't understand why we waited. And he'll believe *you*. If *I* told him, he'd say I imagined it."

"Suppose someone is out there? I don't want to go out in the dark. Besides, you'd be alone. Adeline's in the main house. I came out just to check on you—"

"Oh, Lord. I wish we had a telephone here."

"We'll tell him in the morning."

She had no choice. Zee was right. They couldn't even lock the annex. There were no keys.

For a long time she couldn't sleep. Confusion swirled around her like something tangible. The room expanded, enlarging like a balloon with a distant dome and then disappearing entirely. She was airborne, rushing through space with the sound of whispers and music boxes all around her. She tried to hold herself down but the currents were too strong. Even her cries for help were lost in the whirling wind. Finally she left all human contact behind as she continued hurling toward some distant universe.

11

For a moment after awakening she had the familiar sensation that it had all been a dream, and then she realized Zee had heard it also. Glancing at her watch, she saw that it was too early to call her, so she waited, watching the shell-like pink of the morning sky. From the open window came all the fragrances of new life.

By eight-thirty she wondered why Zee wasn't up yet. Breakfast was served at nine and Gillian didn't like stragglers. Finally she called, but there was no answer. Perhaps Zee had gone out early to telephone the doctor about what had happened. In a loud voice she called for Adeline, but again there was no answer. The only one who showed up was Beth, who stood in the doorway babbling. To get rid of her, she gave her a small china egg which had been among her belongings, and Beth staggered off.

At nine-fifteen, Adeline came back to the annex to see why they hadn't shown up for breakfast.

"Why are you still in bed?" she demanded.

"Because Zee isn't here. I called her but she doesn't answer."

Frowning, Adeline went into Zee's room. There was a moment's silence, and then she returned. She was holding a piece of paper in her hand and she looked stunned.

Instantly Jane's nerves began to sting. She should have known it wouldn't be that easy. "What is it?" she asked in a controlled voice.

Adeline gave her the note. It was short and carelessly written: "I got a better job. I didn't want to tell you. Zee."

Long ago she had been given a paperweight with the usual snow scene. When she shook it, there was the peaceful sprinkling of white on the little New England church. But then she had broken it, and whenever she turned it, there was only a mass of confusion. That's what had happened to her serene, half-asleep existence. It was a mass of confusion.

"She wouldn't do that," Jane whispered.

"I thought she liked it here," Adeline agreed.

"Are her clothes and things gone?"

"Every stitch."

The two of them stared at one another. Finally Jane sat up and said, "Could you please help me get dressed? I have to see the doctor." As soon as the words were out, she was fearful again. *Don't tell anyone about tonight, Jane. We'll be watching you. If you tell—*

And what could she tell him? That she had heard a voice and music coming from nowhere? She could picture his reaction.

Aloud she said, "No, I guess I won't see the doctor. I'll have breakfast." Numbly she allowed herself to be helped through the morning ritual and wheeled to the dining room. Slowly she was beginning to realize how dependent she had been upon Zee, not only physically, but emotionally. She had enjoyed the trivial stories about Gib, the uncomplicated chatter, the lively, superficial interests.

Had she dreamed it or hadn't she? Her mind was reverting to fuzziness again. Was it possible that, in the course of all those operations, they had removed something, a tiny particle of gray matter? She had read that it was a procedure followed in some cases of mental derangement. And, of course, the patient would never realize it.

Another thought occurred to her. Absorbed in her own preoccupations with whether or not she had imagined the voice, she had forgotten Zee's possible plight. If it had *not* been a dream, and if she could trust her own instinct that Zee, for all her faults, wouldn't abandon her without notice, then something terrible might be happening to Zee.

But why Zee? Wouldn't it have been simpler to get rid of Jane Wallcutt? She had no answer for that.

"I just heard the bad news."

It was the doctor. She examined him silently for a moment, trying to make up her mind. If she spoke, she might be endangering her own life; if she didn't, Zee's. Slowly, speaking as though to a child, she told him the whole story. Her voice was flat and without emotion.

He was silent for a long time. When he began to light a cigarette, she knew it was hopeless. He always smoked when he was embarrassed or trying to fill an awkward pause.

Finally she said, "Well, you will admit it was lictious of Zee to disappear right after it happened."

"Lictious? Oh—you mean suspicious."

"Well—wasn't it?"

"Jane—listen. You've had a shock. What Zee did was inexcusable. You've been dependent upon her ever since you can remember. And her leaving you like this, suddenly, without warning, made you—uh—sometimes the mind provides excuses. You couldn't bear the thought that she might have left you because she didn't like it here—so unconsciously you tried to find a reason—"

"Oh God," she said, and shut her eyes.

"Please don't feel upset. I was talking to Gillian about it. She pointed out that people uh—like Zee are often irresponsible. Don't think it's your fault—"

"Do you have a sample of Zee's handwriting?"

"Zee's handwriting? Oh—I see. The note. Well—no, that is, I don't think so. As I was saying—"

"Dr. Stires—I wonder—I don't mean to be rude, but I feel awful. I wonder if you could—that is, I want to be alone."

He continued smoking silently for a while longer. Finally he got up, started to say something, changed his mind and left. Too depressed to do anything, even read, she remained where she was. She wondered if he had arranged for another nurse. Then she wondered if she could possibly use the telephone to call the police. It was useless. For one thing, there was only one telephone, smack in the front hall, and everyone would know what she was doing. For another thing, they wouldn't believe her.

She would really be much better off dead. It was all too much for her, and she was only a remnant of a human being anyway. She couldn't walk and she couldn't remember. A quivering, useless remnant of humanity. If she had any courage she would kill herself.

Perhaps that was what they wanted. For her to commit suicide. It was much better than an "accident." The trouble with suicide, however, was that it pleased one's enemies and hurt one's friends. Did she have any friends? The thought of Austin floated into her mind, but she dismissed it. He was an enigma as far as she was concerned. Or they might be trying to drive her out of her mind, or convince the doctor that she was out of her mind. If that was it, they had already more than half succeeded. The third possibility was that they wanted to frighten her away from the sanitarium so that they could arrange for a more convincing accident. Surely they couldn't try a hunter's bullet again.

There was a knock on the door. Her first reaction was fear, but then she realized that no one intent upon hurting her would knock. "Come in."

The man was a stranger, but she wasn't alarmed. In some inexplicable way, it was as though someone had opened the door to her dungeon and let in the sun. Instead of the blackness, the dampness, the scurrying of small, vile things, there was the smell of hay and the warmth of daylight.

"How are you, my dear?" he asked, and it wasn't that she remembered *him*, but people like him—ordinary, well-meaning, educated, and moneyed. He left the door open as though to make sure of the proprieties, and then, placing his hat carefully on the chest of drawers, he asked, "May I sit down?"

"Yes—of course."

He sat queasily, as though distrusting the cleanliness of the chair, and asked, "Do you remember me?"

She examined him carefully, and noticing that she seemed to

be having trouble with her eyes, he leaned forward obligingly. He was somewhat over medium height, portly, and yet with smallish features for someone of his size. The effect was a trifle comic, as though he had been made by someone with a poor sense of proportion. But, of course, she had been exposed to so many badly made people recently, it was picayune to quibble about so small a fault.

"No. I'm sorry."

"The doctor warned me, of course, but I couldn't quite—I thought once you saw me, it would come back. It's unbelievable —don't I seem the least bit familiar?"

"No—I'm afraid not."

"Howard Chalmers. Does the *name* ring a bell?"

She wished he would stop hammering at her. Who had mentioned that name recently?

"Try," he coaxed. Apparently he was convinced that loss of memory was due to lack of effort. "You can do anything if you try. Remember how I told you that all your life?"

"You're the trustee!"

"You remember!" he exclaimed triumphantly. Then doubt crept into his voice. "*The* trustee? Not *my* trustee. Not Uncle Howard."

"No, I don't remember. But when you said that about 'all your life' I knew you must be the—my trustee. Dr. Stires mentioned you."

"Oh." He was disappointed. "Incredible. One reads about these things—but to have someone who's been like a daughter to you not recognize you—"

Helplessly she said, "I didn't even recognize the—uh, my fiancé."

"But Austin was involved in your memory of that terrible experience. I can understand your not wanting to remember *him*. But I—I go back to your childhood, to your earliest, your happiest memories."

He went on at length, reminding her of Zee in that respect,

about some distant anecdotes involving Hobe Sound or some such place, and while he spoke, she tried to tailor him for the role of villain. Suppose he had assumed, at first, that she would die, would he have taken a chance on siphoning off her money? She noted the well-fitted suit, the soft, polished shoes, the dark, perfect hat. He was as prosperous-looking as the man in the Cadillac, but with a huge difference. Obviously he had had the best since birth. Then, if he had lost his money in some manner, mightn't he be more tempted than someone else to find another source? And wasn't it odd that he had arrived in the middle of the week just after Zee disappeared? The sanitarium was quite far from the city, and Austin had told her it would be hard to manage a visit except on weekends.

"How did you happen to get away from work today?" she asked abruptly, not realizing until it was too late that she had interrupted something about "—little dinghy and tried to get us out. Pardon me?"

"I'm sorry," she said in confusion, and this time she wondered if she *did* remember him, because she found herself sliding backward in time to an age when grownups were continuously saying things like, "Children should be seen and not heard."

"I'm sorry. I didn't realize—I was wondering how you managed to leave your office—it must be driff—diff—oh, I can't get the word—" Desperately she said, "I mean, how did you get away from work during the week?"

He smiled indulgently. "Really, my dear, I don't go to work on a nine-to-five basis. Austin told me you were ready for visitors, and I didn't want to interfere with *his* time on weekends."

"Oh—it was kind of you."

"*Kind* of me! You've been like a daughter to me for nearly twenty years— Never mind. Let's get down to business. You must tell me what you need and if you're happy here—that is, as happy as possible under the circumstances. When you're stronger, we can have a chat about your business affairs—"

"Do I have a lot of money?" she interrupted again and turned red.

"Everything is relative," he said pontifically, "but I would say that most people would consider it quite a lot."

"How much do I have?"

He laughed. "You're getting more like yourself every minute. It's not that simple. Aside from the money left to you by your grandfather on your mother's side, and your grandmother on your father's side—"

"It sounds like a song."

"What? Oh. Well, aside from that, there's the money your mother left. The estate hasn't been settled yet. In addition there are trust funds and various kinds of securities—"

"Could you give me—well, a round figure?"

"It's nearly impossible. There are so many factors. And you realize, of course, that if I did give you a round figure, it wouldn't actually represent money you could touch. You have an income, of course, a very generous one, but there are restrictions on the capital. And I'm not your only trustee. There are three of us—"

"Three?"

"Your father was far too good a businessman to put everything in the hands of one person. I'm the only one who was a personal friend of his, but the money is handled so that if one of us dies—"

"I see," she said slowly. How could the money be mismanaged if there were three of them? Unless all three were plotting—

"If you could just give me some idea of what I'm worth."

"Well, as near as I can estimate it at the moment you may be worth about thirteen million doll—"

"Thirteen million!" she exclaimed incredulously.

"Does that surprise you?"

"My Lord!"

"But you must have had some idea— I keep forgetting. You seem so normal."

She had stopped listening. She had the answer to the question about why it was not simpler to get rid of Jane Wallcutt rather

than poor Zee. The disappearance of a nurse would never cause
the furor occasioned by the disappearance of an heiress. Her own
death would *have* to look accidental.

He was talking about her coming to live with him as soon
as she was better. "I mean, at least until you can stand on your
own feet—" He glanced at her legs and then away. "You don't
own a house anymore, and it's the only sensible thing to do. Of
course, Austin may be making plans—" He smiled jovially at her.

Something lurched in her chest. She still wasn't sure whether
or not Austin would show up Saturday, and in spite of the fear,
she felt she couldn't go through another week if he didn't. "Austin's plans may not include me," she said tentatively.

"Nonsense. You two may have had a little trouble, but all engaged couples—"

"What kind of trouble?"

"How would *I* know. Young people never tell their elders anything. The doctor said I wasn't to tire you out. I'll come back
in the middle of next week. Tell me what to bring you. What
would you like most?"

"For you to tell me about the trouble between Austin and me."

"I don't know. Oh here, I almost forgot. I thought you might
need some money. I know everything here is taken care of, but
now that you're getting along so well, you might want money."
He took a small foldover checkbook from his breast pocket and
gave it to her. "I started you off with a thousand dollars. Of
course, if you need more, telephone me. They have my number."

He either couldn't or wouldn't tell her anything more about
Austin. She had misjudged him. He had seemed, at first, an easy-
to-manage kind of person, but now he struck her as hard to
move. Certainly he could never be made to do anything or say
anything he didn't want to do or say. She held out her hand as he
rose, and he took it. Unexpectedly, he bent and kissed her cheek,
and a flash of warmth shot through her. It was the first kiss she
remembered. His pontifical manner no longer irritating her, she
reached up impulsively and kissed him back. He seemed a little

embarrassed, but touched. Brusquely, his voice hoarse, he said, "Everything is going to be all right, Janie," and he patted her hand and went out quickly. She had seen the moisture in his eyes just before he had turned.

The elevator of her spirits lifted again. She was no longer alone. She hadn't had this reaction after Austin's visit. Then there had been a submerged excitement, but this time she had a sense of family, of being loved. She felt the tears on her own cheeks and brushed them away impatiently. You ass, she told herself.

He hadn't closed the door completely, and it began to open slowly. It was Bonnie. Nodding and grinning, she peered at Jane through her small slit eyes and showed her the usual collection of assorted envelopes, circulars, scraps of discarded paper. She waved her stick around, and afraid she would be hit, Jane caught the end and put it down on the bed. Then, obligingly, she began to inspect Bonnie's treasures. About to return them, she saw that one scrap was part of a personal letter. The word "accident" caught her eye, and without thinking, she lifted it to read it. Bonnie jabbered excitedly and Jane promised to return it. It was written on ordinary white stationery, and all she seemed to have of it was the lower right hand corner:

————tter of time
————g to ask questions
————e can't do any————
————spital, but we
————best plan is to keep
————ntime have Leroy scare
————When she gets out
————me for an accident.

She stared at the scrap of paper for a long time, conscious of her growing uneasiness. It could have been in Bonnie's possession for years, she reminded herself, but it looked too clean.

Quickly she spread the other papers out to see if she could find the rest of the letter, but she saw nothing that fit.

What did it mean? Someone here had received a letter that mentioned "an accident" and Bonnie had either grabbed part of it, or found it. What of it? Jane didn't have a monopoly on accidents.

"———ntime have Leroy scare———"

Leroy scare who? Her? The man in the Cadillac—was he Leroy?

"———spital" must be hospital.

What was "———tter of time"? Letter? It made no sense. She had it. "A matter of time."

"———e can't do any———" He? We? We can't do anything.

"When she gets out" and then "an accident."

You're out of your mind, she told herself. That's what they would say if you tried to show them this and said it was a plot against you.

Bonnie was still jabbering and making frantic efforts to retrieve the piece of paper. Looking around, Jane saw the checkbook, tore out a blank check and gave it to Bonnie in lieu of the other treasure. Distracted, the dwarf accepted it and Jane hid the letter under her pillow.

12

When the car purred up the driveway, her throat was dry as sand and she was afraid she would be unable to stammer a greeting. He had called the day before to ask the doctor's permission to take her out to dinner, and ever since she had been in a feverish state.

He waved to her, and turning to Gillian, who hadn't been able to resist coming out again, said rather elaborately, "Hello, Mrs. Simpson. It's nice to see you again."

"Hello, Mr. Berquist. It's lucky you don't come too often or Jane would have a nervous breakdown. You should have seen her. She changed her clothes three times because she couldn't find anything good enough. Was she always like this when you used to take her out in the old days?"

"Constantly. I'd have to give her sedatives before a date."

She would gladly have killed Gillian. Examining her nails, she tried to think of some offhand remark to take the curse off Gillian's revelations, but she was still at it when suddenly he put one arm around her shoulders, the other under her knees, and lifted her. She hadn't even considered her mode of transportation, and she was overcome with a mixture of embarrassment and something else. To hold on, she had to reach around his neck, and she had an almost irresistible desire to shut her eyes and kiss him. Instead she was rigid, keeping as far away as possible.

"Have a good time," Gillian called, adding coyly, "but not too good a time."

Some of her irritation vanished and she was sorry for poor Gillian who had nothing to look forward to. As they drove along, she kept sniffing the air and examining the countryside, pretending a great interest in everything, and delivering a flock of inane comments. He glanced at her occasionally, as though puzzled, but contributed little. They passed a golf course with brightly colored figures dotting the green like wild flowers; a village buzzing with late-shopping women and children; teen-agers racing back and forth as haphazardly as May flies; cows and sheep grazing with their young. It was the latter which made her say suddenly, "They're like us—they don't know they're being fatted for the kill."

This time she met his eyes when he glanced at her, and was taken aback at the intensity of his stare. He seemed about to ask her something, but instead said lightly, "The way I look at it, is, isn't it wonderful the way life renews itself—the calf beside the cow, the buds on the trees, the paint on the church—"

"The paint on the church! Do you really think it renews *itself?*"

"That's the difference between you pessimists and us optimists."

"You know, I feel like that Tsar what's-his-name—what *was* his name?"

"All tsars were called Nicholas."

"Yes. I feel like Tsar Nicholas who drove through the country-side for the first time to see how his subjects were getting along. And everything looked very prosperous, but actually his men had painted the front of the farm buildings and given a few of the peasants new clothing and told them to dance and look happy. While inside the houses, the children were dying of hunger—"

"You do have the damnedest memories!"

"Well, to be perfectly honest, I don't actually *remember* Tsar Nicholas. I read about him."

"I rather suspected it. Surgery is wonderful, but not that wonderful."

"You know you have the damnedest way of being tactless. Were you always this tactless?"

"Well," he said judiciously, "you can't make a lobster cantonese out of a lobster thermidor."

When that made her laugh, he said, "There's a lot to this loss of memory business. I can bring out all my old jokes."

"I guess the reason I remember history is—well, the doctor said I was apt to remember anything I wanted to remember, and forget everything that was unpleasant."

"And there was nothing pleasanter than old Tsar what's-his-name and nothing unpleasanter than me."

"Austin, we weren't engaged when the accident occurred. Why?"

He slowed down to study a sign and turned left. "How do you know?"

"I wasn't wearing a ring."

"You had returned it to me at dinner. For the second or third time. I said that since I'd already bought the tickets, we might just as well see the play anyway." Almost to himself he added, "If you'd been a little less civilized, if you'd shouted at me and walked off, we wouldn't have gone—"

"Why did I return the ring? Did we have an argument?"

"One of many," he said absently. "I wonder how many people missed the show that night because of some little thing—an argument or a headache or a cold. And then gave the ticket to some unfortunate relative or friend who—"

Feeling chilled, she said doggedly, "What did we argue about?"

"I don't remember—oh yes. You'd met an old boy friend the evening before and gone to a party with him. I said engaged girls didn't go to parties with other men, and you said he wasn't a man, he was an old friend. And I said I didn't really mind except that I hated to think of you doing with someone else what you did with me—arguing, nagging, complaining—" He seemed to have worked himself up thinking about it, and then, realizing what he was doing, broke off. "Oh well," he said lightly. "Water over the dam. Spilt milk—"

"Don't lock the barn door," she assented.

He veered sharply to avoid a carful of teenagers which nearly ran them down. "The local natives are out in force today."

"It's the cars. They're full of new innovations."

"The consensus of opinion is that all teenagers ought to be put into hibernation until they grow up."

"I'm running out," she said laughing helplessly.

He turned to look at her and they both smiled, but gradually the smiles turned to something else. She felt confused, and then, in spite of the fact that she had tried to divert him only a moment before, she said, "What happened to *you* the night of the fire?" She'd had no idea that the question was propagating until it sprouted.

Something about his face made her remember the dream in which her mother had warned her against him.

"Nothing very much," he said finally. "I suppose if I had been a quicker thinker I could have gotten you out in time. But I wasn't very decisive. Some people had the sense to get up and leave as soon as they smelled smoke. But you and I—we were the kind who thought it wasn't nice to panic." He stopped talking to her and began talking to himself. *"Nice!* There wasn't much niceness in that theater that night. It was the most ugly— but I shouldn't say that. Some people were—there's no word for it. In wars, they're the ones who become winners of Congressional Medals of Honor. I remember one man—a character who shouted 'siddown' at the beginning to avoid a stampede—he kept trying to calm them, right to the end. I saw him grabbing children and tossing them to another man on a kind of chain—I don't know if you remember—no, of course you don't—it was the kind of show you could take children to. Anyway, he was near an exit himself, but he never made a move toward it—he was too busy—I don't know what happened to him . . ."

He stopped, his skin yellow under the tan, and faint lines appeared around his mouth and eyes.

"I'd rather not hear any more about it," she said.

"It was unbelievable. I mean—I'd read about things like that, but I never—I couldn't imagine people could behave like that. Two old people—the man tried to help her—they never had a chance. And then, this woman with a kid—I tried to grab them, but the kid was wrenched away, I don't know how—maybe someone grabbed him to keep from falling—and then the balcony gave way—it broke in two—you went down first—I saw you going—but I couldn't—it all happened so quickly. No—it was all too slow—" He took a deep breath and finished passionately, "I hope you *never* remember."

She was gripping her hands together so tightly, the nails bit into her palm and the knuckles turned white. A machine hummed in her brain as though an engine in a vast subterranean chamber was grinding out some unspeakable product.

"And then, my part of the balcony collapsed too. It went down on top of yours, I think. I remember falling and thinking, "Thank God, it's over—" An odd expression crossed his face, wiping away all the emotion, as though he'd just recalled a fact which made everything he'd said invalid. More matter-of-factly, he said, "When I woke up I was in a hospital. It was the quiet that impressed me more than anything. After all those terrible— and the nothing. White walls, clean sheets, soft voices in the hall—and I was hardly hurt. Some burns and a few broken ribs. It was freakish. A matter of where one was sitting and how one fell. People next to one another were completely—that is, they met completely different fates.

"Anyway, I asked about you, of course. At that time they weren't sure you were going to make it at all. Aside from the fall, you had more than fifty percent of your body burned. If I hadn't—"

"Stop it," she said. She was surprised at the softness of her voice. She had thought it would be a scream. She began putting her hands to her ears—to blot out not the screams, but the sound of the machinery—and then she made an effort and kept her hands on her lap.

"Okay," he said abruptly. "I like the suit you're wearing. That's always a safe topic."

She looked down at her white wool suit. Slowly she said, "You sound uh—what's the word? Are you implying I've always been overly interested in clothing?"

"You mean you don't remember *that?* Then it hasn't all been in vain. I think I'll take up brain surgery and remove parts for things like interest in clothing. 'And what's *your* profession, Mr. Berquist?' 'Well, I'm a part-time brain surgeon. I specialize in minor operations. Nice clean work—'

" 'No washing up yourself. Garbage disposal for unwanted bits and pieces—'

"Housewives of America, what are *you* doing with your spare time? Become part-time brain surgeons, heart specialists—

"Take our ten-week correspondence course. Results guaranteed. Complete satisfaction or we return the bits of the brain we removed." The sound of the machinery had diminished, as though they were leaving that part of the world where the underground work was going on. She had one last thought on the subject. When the fire became one of those famous disasters in which the survivors congregated yearly to recount their experiences, she would be the only one who would be unable to contribute anything.

Aloud she was telling him, "Everything is wrong. I've lost weight and the styles have changed. Even the shoes are wrong. They're wearing them more square-toed now and low-heeled—"

"Fascinating. Simply fascinating. Now, in men's clothing, the lapels have been narrowed by one sixteenth of an inch, and I understand that the slit down the back—if you'll pardon the expression—is entirely out of step with fashion. The cuffs are turned back just a smidgen—" He turned off the road into a driveway. At first she thought he was taking her to a large, private house, but then she saw the discreet sign announcing that they were at The Revere Inn. He lifted her in his arms again and they passed a stream with chairs and tables on the bank, but he carried her indoors to a table for four near a massive stone fireplace. The room was dimly lit, and the atmosphere was all early American—dark beams, pewter mugs on display, portraits of pioneers.

They were barely seated when a man and a woman approached from the direction of the bar, and Austin rose again. Without a word, he held one of the chairs for the woman, and the couple seated themselves. Jane looked at Austin inquiringly and met an intent, searching stare. But even then she didn't understand and smiled uncertainly at the two apparent intruders.

"Jane, honey, don't you remember me at all?" the woman wailed, and finally she understood. Austin was using shock tactics.

"I'm sorry," she said stonily. Disappointment that they wouldn't be alone made it hard for her to speak.

The woman took Jane's hand and patted it. "Never mind. It wasn't such a hot idea anyway."

"Liz and Fred Dickinson," Austin said. "They're old friends. You went to school with Liz."

"Janie," Fred Dickinson said, "I told these two characters you ought to be warned."

"It's perfectly all right," she said. Something was lodged in her throat and she took a sip of water. The other three began to talk, as though giving her time to collect herself, but she sensed that, although Austin addressed his remarks to Liz and Fred, his attention was on her.

After a while she realized that Liz, like everyone else she had met recently, was reconstructing another part of her past for her. "—awful pill back then. I don't mind telling you. I'm not going to start being polite at this late date. I always felt so awkward and gawky with you around. Actually I'm not that much taller than you are, but you were so adorable, so well coordinated, everyone always thought I was a giant compared to you. You could do *anything*. Anything important, that is, like play hockey and swim and beat everyone in tennis and golf. All I could do was get better grades than you. And that was because you didn't care. The boys would tell me what a classic face I had and then they'd ask *you* for a date."

The waiter arrived and Austin ordered drinks without consulting her. As though they were afraid of the quiet, Fred took up the ball as soon as Liz dropped it. "Liz didn't even introduce me to you until I had asked her to marry me. She figured it was too late for me to get out of it."

"They've done a remarkable job, Jane," Liz said. "You look marvelous."

Her husband groaned.

"It's all right," Jane assured him. "I want you all to act natural."

"See?" Liz said. "I was sure she didn't want to be treated like delicate china. I bet everyone—"

"Actually," she said carefully, "*no one* has treated me like delicate china."

"—has been tiptoeing around. Well, if you're referring to Austin, he always was rather rude. Anyway, you look wonderful. And I think that what happened to your vocal chords is an improvement. I like that husky quality. Austin says you'll be able to walk again soon. I hope you're no good at sports though. I'd love to beat you at tennis."

Fred rolled his eyeballs at Austin, but just then the drinks arrived. She saw a stemmed glass with a colorless liquid in it. There was also a relish tray of radishes and olives, and a basket of hot, crunchy bread. "Skoal," Liz said, and Jane took a large gulp of her drink. She blinked and set it down. "You know what? There's been something missing in my life, and at last I know what it is."

They all laughed and Austin said, "She's getting more like herself every minute."

She took deep gulps of air, as though trying to absorb everything: the food, the atmosphere of the inn, the people she was with, the clothing, the scraps of conversation she overheard ("But darling, at my age, only two things are important, money and power."), even the smell of the wood-burning fire.

"What will you have?" Austin asked, after ordering another round of drinks.

"I don't know. Order what I used to love most."

"You were always dieting. But all right." To the waiter, he said, "Roast beef with whatever green vegetable you have, no potatoes."

"Oh, how dull. Never mind. I'll do my own ordering. I'll have that trout in butter sauce and the lobster and french fries."

Liz raised her eyebrows. "Keep eating like that and *no* one will look at you again."

"There's someone looking at her right now," Fred said, glancing over Jane's shoulder.

She felt a warning tingle in her spine. Turning quickly she tried to see who it was, but her vision was blurred. "Who's looking at me?"

"That man over there. He just got up and he's going into the other room."

"What was he like?"

Austin, who had finished ordering, said, "Come on. You're not *that* starved for attention."

"Men always looked at you, sweetie," Liz added, puzzled.

"Please—I can't explain. Describe him."

"Oh—I don't know, kind of sharp."

"You mean well dressed?"

"Well—tastes differ, but—"

"Was he blond and kind of small?"

"I didn't take that close a look—I didn't think you'd get this upset. The man was going by and he simply happened to turn around and look—"

"You said he got up and went into the other room when we turned to look at him. I'm going to the ladies room so that I can pass his tab— Oh, I forgot. I can't." She stared at them helplessly and they all began to laugh. "What will I do if I— Austin can't carry me."

"It's a problem," he admitted.

She was distracted by the arrival of her first course. Once more she peered around, but everything was a blur, and she gave up and began to eat. "This is heavenly," she said. She ate as though she hadn't seen food for years and they all made frank comments. "Sorry," she said. "But you must remember I've had nothing but casseroles ever since I can remember."

"I can't wait to start you on French food," he said as though she were a newborn baby. She glanced at him quickly but he was busy lighting a cigarette.

By the time she had finished and was washing her fingers in the bowl, the combination of the unaccustomed drinks and the fact that she was with her oldest friends overcame her caution and she reached into her purse. "Look at this," she said, showing them the scrap of paper she had pilfered from Bonnie.

Austin examined it, turned it over to see if there was anything further on the back and then handed it to Fred. "What about it?" he asked, puzzled.

She had expected more of a reaction, and something began to flutter in her chest. Hesitantly she said, "I found it in Bonnie's junk. She's the patient who—the dwarf—she picks things up from wastebaskets and takes things from people's pockets—"

"Yes?"

She found herself beginning to stammer. "Well, doesn't it sound uh—renting?"

The other three carefully avoided exchanging glances. In a neutral voice Austin said, "I think you mean threatening."

"Yes." She hated the note of apology which crept into her voice. "I still have some difficulty with words. I'm not really explaining this right. But I've got to confide in someone and you three—" She looked at them imploringly, but the easy camaraderie of a moment before was gone. They seemed baffled, and she wished she hadn't brought up the subject. But now that she had, she felt that she had to explain. "You see," she said quickly, "the other day, a man like the one Fred said was staring at me—"

Carefully Fred said, "I didn't say he was staring. I said he looked at you."

"Oh. Well, yes. A small blond man came to the sanitarium and he said some odd things."

"Who was he?" Austin asked.

"I don't know."

"What did he say?"

"It's hard to remember. Let me see. He was kind of threatening—"

"He *threatened* you?"

"No, not exactly. But he seemed—well, he knew, for instance, that I'd lost my memory—"

"He was probably related to one of the other patients who had told him—"

"No. He spoke to no one else. Just me. He said I was only pretending to lose my memory—"

"Why should you do a thing like that?" Liz asked. Abruptly Austin seemed to have lost interest. He began pouring more coffee for everyone.

"How should *I* know? Then he said something about the sanitarium being much nicer than fires and accidents—"

"Jane," Austin said, and something in his voice made her look at him, but his attention was on the coffee pot. "You're simply not making sense."

She was unaccountably frightened. Their faces upset her.

"It's true," she said, her voice rising. "He warned me that something would happen if I remembered anything from before the accident."

"Take it easy. Why shouldn't you remember anything?"

"How should I know? He said he had spies watching me—"

"He told you that? He actually said he had spies?"

"No, not exactly. He said he had friends everywhere—"

"Well, that's not the same as spies."

"You're confusing me. You act as though I'm crazy."

The three looked oddly alike. As though their faces had been scrubbed clean of all expression.

"He was awful. I mean—I can't point to anything specific, but everything about him was rolving—"

"What?" asked Fred.

"I think she means revolting," Austin explained in the same neutral tone.

His aloofness made her desperate. She had to break through it. "Yes, revolting. I can't help it if I lose a word now and then. But I'm sane. He threatened me, I tell you. He wasn't specific, but I could feel it. Didn't you ever sense evil in someone?"

She was building a wall around herself, she saw. Austin drank some coffee and said, "Suppose I talk to Dr. Stires and—"

"He didn't believe me either. And the only one who heard the voice and would believe me is—"

She stopped dead. She hadn't meant to reveal anything about the music or the voice. If they behaved this way about a note they could see, how would they react to a story about a voice?

"The voice?" Liz was saying.

"Oh God—I didn't mean to tell you about that. I knew you'd *really* think I was crazy—Zee heard it, and now she's disappeared."

"Perhaps you'd better start at the beginning." It was Austin.

"What's the use." She looked around. Everyone else seemed to be having a marvelous time. Only their table was the center of a vacuum, a dead place in which nothing moved. Well, yes, one thing did, an evil, slithering shadow coming closer and closer and visible only to herself. Dully she said, "I woke up the other night and I heard music. It was a music box. Oh—I know what you're thinking, but I heard it. And then a voice called me. 'Jane, Jane,' just like that, over and over again. It told me not to remember the accident or anything that happened before that. It said I'd be watched and if I remembered or told anyone about it, something awful would happen to me."

She stopped talking and there was dead silence. She felt alone, abandoned in a vast desert, accompanied only by the evil thing. She didn't look at them. She couldn't bear the expressions she knew would be on their faces. She felt tears stinging her eyes and prayed she wouldn't make a fool of herself in public.

Evenly Austin said, "The doctor told me Zee had left. Were you going to say before that she heard this—this voice?"

"Yes, she did. And the next day she was gone."

"But dear," Liz said delicately, "isn't she—wasn't she uh a Negress? They often behave irresponsibly—"

"Not Zee. She wouldn't. And while I'm at it, I might as well tell you everything. Someone shot at me."

"Shot at you." Austin's voice was as dull as her own.

"Yes, from the woods. It could have been a hunter, of course, but it was awfully close. If I hadn't moved, the bullet would have struck me." Her voice trailed off. She looked at them, and it was as she had expected. Their faces were closed—not hostile, just veiled. It was as though they had twitched back to avoid contact with something unclean.

"I feel like—like an animal staked to a tree near the drinking pool," she said softly. "You know, a lamb used for bait to attract the lion or whatever it is. And pretty soon—pretty soon, the lion will come to the drinking pool."

13

"The funniest thing happened," Gillian said when she arrived Sunday morning to help her get dressed.

She felt an accelerated pumping in her chest.

"Zee's sister called last night after you left. You know—Gib's mother?"

"Yes?" She was careful to keep her voice even.

"She wanted to know why Zee didn't show up Saturday night as usual."

She shut her eyes for a moment and passively allowed herself to be helped into the wheel chair. While Gillian discussed the possibilities (Zee had run off with a man; Zee had absconded with money), she tried to think.

"Did you tell the doctor?" she asked in the middle of something Gillian was saying.

"Personally," Gillian said ungrammatically but good-naturedly, "you don't have very good manners. I was talking and you interrupted."

"I'm sorry. It's important."

"Do you think I'm crazy? What would the doctor say if I called him this early Sunday morning to tell him Zee didn't get home last night? Especially since she left you anyway."

"He ought to know," she insisted.

"What are you so excited about? I'll tell him later."

"Listen, Gillian, please do something for me. Telephone Zee's sister and tell her to call the police—the missing persons bureau right away. Oh God, I hope it's not too late."

"Are you crazy?" Gillian asked in astonishment. "I can just see me calling Zee's sister and telling her to call the police. Don't you know that Zee's kind are always missing? I have no prejudice, God knows, and Zee was a nice girl—she never took advantage—but she is what she is, and nobody can change it."

Tiredly Jane said, "Would you do me that one little favor? Please?"

"Honestly, I'd like to, Jane, but I can't. I'll tell the doctor though." Still chattering she wheeled her into the breakfast room and then she bustled about her work. Afterwards Jane pushed herself outdoors and watched the chickadees on the lawn. The Sunday newspapers hadn't arrived yet and she had forgotten to supply herself with a book before leaving her room. Visions, scraps of conversations, smells, even tastes assailed her, floated around her, trying to anchor her mind to a memory. The patterns in her head were like an intricate mosaic, a blend of colors and detailed designs, growing more interesting under observation.

"The damnedest memories," Austin had said. "You do have the damnedest memories." What had he been talking about? Oh yes, history.

"Look at his history," her mother was saying. "You can't ignore it. Why, even at the age of fourteen—"

But it petered out. At the age of fourteen, what? What had they been discussing?

A movement, just out of the range of her vision, made her turn nervously. But she saw nothing. It was probably a bird.

What had happened to Zee? And what was going to happen to *her*? If they came at night, and particularly if they drugged her first, she wouldn't be able to call for help—

Drugged.

That's what her mother had been saying. "Why, even at the age of fourteen, he was mixed up with a gang selling drugs."

"*Gang? Drugs?* He was in prep school, not on the streets of—"

"It shows how basically wrong he was from the very first. He was expelled from that school and only got into another one because his uncle made a large donation—"

"How do you know all this?"

"I heard it from a woman whose son went to the same school. Then, later on, he started getting involved in these odd organizations, read—"

What did that mean? Odd organizations, read?

With the suddenness of lightning flickering, she was overcome by a sense of urgency. There was something she ought to be doing, someone she ought to be calling. The feeling wasn't new; it went far back—it was as though she had gone to sleep knowing she had a momentous call to make the following day and then awakened, the sense of urgency intact, but the knowledge of whom to call gone.

"They would make calls at night." It was her mother speaking again. How easily the voice was triggered. "It was one of his recreations when he was young—calling people at three or four in the morning and saying ugly things. He's filled with hate— listen to him. He hates so many people and so many things. In ordinary hoodlums, it takes the form of muggings and senseless killings. In people with his background, it takes the form of joining organizations which are on the fringe, just acceptable enough to put a gloss on the crimes he would like to commit . . ."

Gillian's daughter, Adeline, came out wheeling Helen, the spastic paraplegic, and placed her in a protected section of the lawn, covered her with a blanket, and left. What had some mother felt when she found out she had given birth to *that*, Jane wondered. And why had they lavished all this care on it all these years?

The thought frightened her, reminding her of another voice, not her mother's this time. "What good are they? Think how it would improve the human race to eliminate genes like that."

"But who are *you* to say who is to be eliminated? And where would it stop? I mean, it could start with people like that, but then—"

It seemed to Jane that a muscle had moved on Helen's face. Was it possible that thought processes were locked in that brain? Perhaps she was like the soldier who had lost his arms, legs, sight, hearing, tongue—everything but the brain grinding on and on. Wouldn't it be better to be dead?

Followed by Hopeless, Dick ambled by, smiling to himself. The dog sniffed at Dick's heels, but the latter ignored him. It occurred to her that she had never seen any of the patients pick up the dog, or show affection for any animal. Even Marlene seemed to feed the birds out of some dim memory of her duty to the world. It was the right thing to do, like going to church. And yet, she could attend almost any social event and pass for normal.

"Your fiancé called." She looked up. It was the doctor. "He said he would be unable to come up here this weekend."

The blow was almost unbearable. First Zee, now Austin. She was being abandoned by everyone. The people who were the most likely to come to believe in her were all being removed like skins from an onion. In Zee's case, she was sure it was involuntary; in Austin's, it was a matter of his having decided she was incurably sick and there was no point in seeing her again.

"He had to attend some business thing in Washington," the doctor was saying.

Dully she asked, "Did you hear about the call from Zee's sister?"

"Yes."

"Did you, by any chance, suggest that she contact the missing persons bureau?"

"As a matter of fact, I did."

She glanced at him, surprised, and saw that he was smiling.

"Does that mean you're beginning to believe me?" she asked.

"I *believe* you," he said with odd emphasis.

"What does *that* mean?"

"It means that I believe you *think* you really heard voices the other night, but—well, in my opinion, it was a particularly vivid dream."

"I see," she said and stared down the road at the empty gate-house. She decided to pursue only the most necessary pathways. "What did Zee's sister say?"

"She said that if she didn't hear from her by tonight, she would notify the police."

"She's waiting for tonight?"

"Look—she's Zee's closest relative. It's up to her to decide."

"I know. There's nothing more you can do. I wonder," she added, more to herself than to him, "if I ought to tell the police everything. With so many people knowing anyway—"

He ran a hand through his hair. "I'm sure you're well protected here. There are always people around. Incidentally, your new nurse will be here tomorrow."

Distracted, she said, "You have a nurse?"

"Yes."

"How did you—I mean where did you get her?"

"Where did I get her? For heaven's sake! Now what?"

"Nothing."

"Your guardian suggested her name, if you want to know. And about the police—I'll call them, but you must be prepared —that is, this *is* a sanitarium. They'll feel the patients are uh— suspect. Of course I'll tell them that your mind is perfectly normal, but still, they'll have to know about the amnesia and the injuries—"

"Oh God," she said so softly he could barely hear her. "I wish there was someone, anyone I could trust. Someone who would believe me—"

"You can trust me, Jane," he said soothingly, but he added nothing about believing her. She felt as though she were trying to run through soft, clinging webs which couldn't hurt her but which kept sticking to her legs, preventing her from moving. "If you really want me to, I'll call the police."

"Tell them—that is, have them come in business suits. Not uniforms. If anyone is watching—"

"Well, I don't know if I can give them sartorial advice, but I'll try."

"Try not to let anyone hear you call— Oh dear, they come in pairs, don't they? It would make anyone suspect—"

"How would you know they come in pairs?"

"What? Oh. Everyone is always asking me how I know something. I can't help what I remember and what I don't. I probably read about it."

"Well—do you want me to call?"

"I just can't—suppose they don't believe me—never mind. Let me think about it some more."

"All right," he said patiently and went on his rounds, starting with Beth. A car stopped at the entranceway and she turned sharply, but it was only Marlene, returning from church. She had been driven by someone from the parish. She stopped at Jane's chair to chat, and forlornly Jane thought, these were her friends, her family, the only people close to her. As she finally rose to change her clothing, Marlene asked, "Will you come to church with me next Sunday?"

"Oh I'm sorry—you know I can't walk—"

"I can get someone to take you."

She felt it was the least she could do for her family and friends. "Yes, I will," she said firmly.

Kirk, spreading a fungicide on the lawn, grinned at Jane as Marlene went up to the house. "You should see her room. It's filled to the ceiling with religious statues and pictures of angels and Bibles. You can't even walk into it. It's a real firetrap. If we ever have a fi— Oh, I'm sorry."

"That's all right," Jane said. "You may mention fires around me."

"I thought perhaps—"

"I can't remember it anyway. That is, at least I think—" Her voice trailed off. Then, brushing her hair off her forehead, she asked, "How did *your* sickness start?" When the words were out she turned blood red. She wasn't sure if she had asked him the question in order to get him off the subject of fires, or because her surroundings, the atmosphere of the hospital, removed all barriers.

He did another turn with the spreader, and she thought he

was going to ignore the question, but then he came back and straightened up, as though his back hurt. She noticed that he was quite good-looking when he improved his posture. "I'm sorry," she apologized. "I don't know what made me ask that."

"It started without warning," he said, like someone who had gone through it so many times he knew it by heart. "As far as I know, there was never anything like it in the family. Then one day it just happened. I had a queer sensation, a light in front of my eyes—and then nothing. I woke up and found myself lying in the street. I could have hurt myself badly but I was with a friend and he stopped my fall. I went to a doctor and had a lot of tests. He told me it was epilepsy."

"Oh," she said helplessly. "But—well, why do you have to stay *here?*"

"Well—it happened when I was about twenty-nine. I'm thirty-four now. I took drugs, and I hoped I might have a fairly normal life. But a year or two after the first attack, it happened again. I was with some friends in a restaurant—there was no warning. It was pretty—well, it wasn't pleasant. I kept on working for another two years—I was a stock broker—but I seemed to forget things and I couldn't concentrate. And then, the third time it happened, I hurt myself pretty badly. I was told it was dangerous to try to carry on as though nothing had happened. I took more tests, went to more doctors, and well, finally—"

"You came here to garden," she said sadly.

He watched her a moment. "It's not so bad."

"What about your family?"

"You mean my parents? My sisters?"

"No. Uh, I mean—are you married?"

"No. I was engaged when it happened the first time, but of course, after that—"

Bonnie came up to her and said very distinctly, "Mail." She was startled. She had never heard the dwarf enunciate clearly before. "She's talking!"

"Oh—she gets a word out now and then."

Hopeless came and sniffed forlornly at Bonnie's heels and Jane whistled and then scooped him up, holding him tightly. The two of them began nuzzling one another, both of them starved for affection. Kirk watched them a moment and then went on with his work. Like a machine, he went back and forth methodically until he had covered the entire lawn. Then he disappeared into the main house.

The figure standing at the gate was like the serpent in some mad garden of Eden. His face was turned in her direction, and he was absolutely motionless as though he had been waiting for her to be alone. She couldn't see his features, but she had no doubt about who it was.

14

He was as perfectly dressed as before, this time in a brown suit, beige shirt and expensive tie with horses cavorting on it. "Hello, Miss Wallcutt."

"How do you know my name?" She started to wheel the chair back, but he was standing behind it, holding on as though to assist her. "I told you I have lots of friends."

Trying not to be obvious about it, she looked around, but everyone within earshot was mindless. "You didn't listen to me," he was saying. "You should listen when people talk."

The fear was rising like a mist around her, but even so she wanted him to commit himself as much as possible, if only to convince *her* that he was really menacing.

"Why don't you ask me what I'm talkin' about?" She remembered that he liked cooperation. He gave the chair a slight shove, not enough to turn it over, but enough to jar her. "Oops, I tripped."

"What are you talking about?" she whispered.

"That's better. It's polite to talk to people when they talk to you. Not just stare. Starin's rude, my mother taught me. Remember I told you not to look for trouble? You bin lookin' for trouble." He rubbed the diamond on his finger and watched it glitter. "I mean you bin talkin' too much. A body can get into a heap a trouble talkin' too much."

"How do you know—I—what makes you think I've been talking? Talking about what?" They were too far from the house for anyone to hear her, but she knew he enjoyed the sound of his own voice and if she could keep him chatting, perhaps Adeline or Gillian might come out.

"I got friends, I keep tellin' you. I want you to meet one of them." He glanced at the Cadillac, and the fear got thick as she realized that this time he was not alone. She wanted to scream but was afraid it would only precipitate violence. And even if it brought help, how could she explain it? He hadn't done anything except suggest that he introduce her to a friend.

"I don't mean *him*," he said. "Another friend. We want you to come for a ride with us."

Her chest pounding, she gave the chair a sudden twist, and he jumped out of the way, cursing. "You near ruined my shoe," he snarled. "What the hell do you think you're doin'?"

"I don't want to go for a ride," she whispered.

He regained some of his composure at the sight of her fear and opened his eyes in mock surprise. "Don't want to go for a ride? It's borin' sittin' around all day. We'll get you back in time for supper. My friend will help carry you—that is, if you're sure you can't walk."

"You know I can't walk, and I'm not going. I don't want a ride. I'm not bored—"

He began wheeling her toward the car and she saw the man within. He was huge and fat. "I won't go. Gill—"

To anyone watching, it would have looked as though he were bending over her to adjust the mechanism of the wheel chair, but actually his shoulder pressed against her mouth as he snapped, "You want to get all the loonies killed? It won't help you to yell, but I might have to hurt a few—"

A car motor sounded and they both turned to see a blue Buick approaching. "You yell and a lotta innocent people goin' to get hurt. Hear?"

"Let me go, please. I don't know what you want—"

"Nothin'. I'm takin' you for a little ride, that's all."

"I won't say anything, I won't tell anyone—"

"Sure you won't. Now just take it easy or—"

The Buick stopped on the driveway in front of the entrance and two elderly people emerged. They glanced incuriously at the small group around the wheel chair and went indoors. Sunday visitors for a patient.

His hand tightened on her shoulder. "That's a good girl. Don't do nothin' and no one will get hurt." Suddenly he whirled around as he felt something on his back. It was Bonnie, waving her cane. Grabbing it, he threw it as far as he could toward the woods. Her small slit eyes regarded him expressionlessly. Quickly he wheeled Jane to the car and put his hands under her arms, brushing her breasts. The fat man was starting out of the car to help when another car turned up the driveway.

From out of a small Volkswagen jumped a tall, red-haired girl with a homely face. Without hesitation she started straight toward them. "Jane! Jane Wallcutt!"

The small man's seething frustration almost charred her. "Watch your step," he muttered.

"How marvelous you look! How do you feel? You don't know how nice it is to see you again. I've been wanting to come for ages but I was told you weren't ready." She took Jane's hands and went on without stopping to take a breath. "Do you recognize me? No, of course you don't. Austin's kept me posted about your progress. He said you were much better but that you still can't remember anything. I'm Gladys Valentine. We worked at the settlement house together. Only I got paid. I was so happy to hear you could have visitors. I came—"

"We're just takin' Jane for a ride, Miss," the little man said politely. He smiled with boyish charm and bowed slightly.

"Oh no! You can't. You simply can't. I spent two and a half hours getting up here—"

Clearing her throat Jane said, "Now that Gladys is here, I—I think I'll skip the ride."

"See bracelet," Beth said, joining the group. "Pretty. My brother sent me. Very nice. Sends me things all the time. Pocketbook, letters—"

His smile unimpaired, the man said, "She'll be back soon. You can take a walk, talk to the doc. We're old friends of the family."

"I don't know when I'll be able to get away again," Gladys Valentine said briskly. "I'm sure Jane can go for a ride another time." She snapped her purse open and both men stiffened, but all she brought out was a small gift-wrapped box. "Austin told me to give this to you since he can't come next week. It's in the nature of a peace offering. Jane, I've got so much to tell you. You won't recognize the old settlement house when you see it again. They've added a wing and painted the outside. I don't know where the money's been coming from, but someone's been generous." As she chatted, she began wheeling Jane's chair toward the main house where the garden furniture was. "And guess what? Marcia's mother came back—from wherever she was—and she said she's remarried and living in Colorado and she's taking Marcia back with her. Of course I'll miss her horribly, but still—"

"All right, Jane," the small man said genially. "No ride today." He walked around, deliberately standing in front of the wheel chair. "I'll tell my friends to look after you while I'm away. They'll keep me posted on how you're gettin' along and what you're doin'. He smiled, bowed again to Gladys, and stepped into the car. As though they were a well-rehearsed team, the other man got in on the driver's side so that both doors slammed at once, and the car roared off.

She leaned back, shutting her eyes. She was as exhausted as though she had been doing violent physical exercise for hours. She would never have come back, she was sure. If Gladys Valentine hadn't arrived when she had— She opened her eyes. The tall red-haired girl was watching her. "Who was that? Are you tired?"

Jane lifted her head as a plane went by, its wings flashing in the sunlight. It drowned out every other sound for a moment, and then it was gone, the chirpings of birds and insects, louder in contrast to the sudden silence. *I'll tell my friends to look after you while I'm away. They'll keep me posted on how you're gettin' along and what you're doin'.*

She took a deep breath and committed herself. "That was a friend of my family's," she said. She turned away from the red-haired girl's eyes and stared at the peaceful fields stretching toward the horizon, where they blended into a pearllike haze.

The newcomer resumed her monologue about the settlement house, telling her about the children and volunteers she had once presumably known. She said something now and then to show that she was listening. She realized that, having missed the opportunity to tell Gladys immediately about the danger she had been in, she had lessened her chance of being believed. Not that it mattered—Austin and the Dickinsons hadn't believed her anyway. She wondered if the "friends" were hidden anywhere within hearing distance at the moment. It didn't seem possible, but she had read somewhere about microphones which could amplify sound an enormous number of times.

"Do you?" the girl was asking.

"Oh—I'm sorry—I didn't—I thought I saw something down the road." She hadn't seen anything, but it was an excuse for her lapse of attention.

"I was asking you if you had made any plans for the future."

"Oh. Well—not really—" Perhaps that was the answer. Go away where no one could find her. No one. Not even Austin. Impossible. She would need money and physical care—certainly her guardian would have to know where to send her checks—anyway, wouldn't she be more vulnerable away from the hospital than in it?

"Is there anything I can bring you the next time I come? Like books or—"

"Thank you, but I have all the books I want—" Suddenly she noticed the gift on her lap. "Oh—I forgot. Do you know that this is the first gift I ever rec—I mean I remember receiving?" Her fingers trembled faintly as she picked up the box, professionally wrapped in white and gold paper. Was it possible that he was giving her the engagement ring again?

She folded the paper and ribbon neatly, opened the box, and took out the tissue-wrapped object within.

It was a gold St. Christopher's medal.

She stared at it a long time. Her reaction puzzled her. She lifted her eyes so that the tears wouldn't spill and waited for her voice to settle down. "Thank him for me," she said finally. "No—perhaps I can get his address and write to him. Did he say—I mean, uh, why did he think I might need this?"

"Need? He didn't say you needed it. It's a present, that's all."

Jane suggested that her guest stay for dinner, an arrangement that was permitted on Sunday, but the girl said that she wanted to get back before dark. When her visitor was gone, she sat still, thinking. What would happen if she told the doctor about the man in the Cadillac? Certainly enough people could vouch for his presence, but still, she could almost project the entire conversation.

What did he do?

He asked me to go for a ride with him.

What of it?

Well, isn't that odd? I don't know him.

How do you know you don't know him?

Well, he threatened me.

What did he say?

He said, let's see—he said I was looking for trouble—talking too much. He said I could get into trouble talking too much.

Talking about what?

About him, for one thing. He said if I didn't go with him he would hurt the "loonies."

He said that?

Yes, he said if I went along no one would get hurt.

Did anyone else hear this?

Well—Bonnie—but of course she can't tell you anything—he didn't actually say anything when Gladys Valentine was here.

Did you tell this Gladys Valentine about him when he left?

No, I was afraid.

Aren't you afraid now?

Yes, but—

There was no point to it. She wheeled herself inside her own room and sat in the growing dimness, doing nothing. Fleetingly she wondered if she ought to put the light on and pretend to be reading so that if anyone saw her, he wouldn't consider this further evidence of her instability. A streak of stubbornness kept her where she was. It's a free country, she told herself, grimacing. If I want to sit in the dark and think, I can damn well sit in the dark and think.

Snatches of memory, bits of flotsam and jetsam from the dim past drifted through her mind.

"You know you're telling a fib."

"No, Dad, honestly it's true."

She was sitting high above the ground on a fence—she could almost taste the bittersweet sting of the fruit—Concord grapes. Her father asking, "Are you sure the Riggses gave you permission to eat their grapes?"

"Sure, Daddy. Honestly."

Honestly. And he had believed her; unlike the doctor he had trusted her word—unjustifiably. Now, no one trusted her. Like the boy who had cried wolf.

Actually nothing was real. There hadn't been a fire, an accident, a hospital, a doctor, Austin, a man in a Cadillac, a bullet, a guardian, a voice, Zee—it was all an illusion. She was a loonie in a loonie bin and nothing was true.

The doctor, passing her door, brought her out of it. "Dr. Stires!" she called.

He veered back and opened the French doors.

"You're here twice today," she said, a question in her voice.

"One of the visitors wanted to see me."

"I just remembered something about my father. I was wondering if you have a description of him. I have quite a clear picture in my mind and I want to check—"

His expression stopped her. "*Now* what have I done wrong?" she asked apprehensively.

"Nothing," he said carefully. "It's just that I doubt very much if you could remember your father. I just found out. He died when you were three months old."

15

The new nurse arrived early Monday morning. She was a tall woman, athletic-looking and in her forties. She had fuzzy hair of no particular style or color, a faintly horselike but aristocratic face, and an educated voice.

For some reason Jane couldn't stop babbling in her presence, in much the same way that she had when Austin had taken her out, but that nervousness had been a pleasurable frenzy. This one was composed completely of uneasiness. "How did you happen to hear about this job?" she asked at one point, sandwiching the question in with others in the hope that it would appear unimportant.

The woman, in the process of efficiently sorting Jane's clothing in separate piles for the laundry, cleaners, and thrift shop, turned slowly, looking at Jane with large, oddly opaque eyes. "Through an agency. Why?"

"Oh. You know. Curiosity. Just making conversation. There isn't much else to do around here. I thought—that is, I had the impression that someone recommended you." With distaste, she noticed how apologetic her own voice sounded.

The nurse turned back to her work.

"Let me see," Jane persisted, "was it the doctor who said someone recommended you?"

"I think you'll be satisfied, Miss Wallcutt. I have excellent references."

Teetering at the edge of a decision, wondering if the end result would justify the antagonism the suggestion might generate, Jane finally plunged. "Could I see some of them?" she asked brightly. "Of course I'm perfectly—uh—that is, I'm sure it will work out—but, you can understand—uh, I had a bad experience once. Someone I—uh hired—"

"I was under the impression that you're suffering from amnesia, Miss Wallcutt."

How had she fallen into this cul-de-sac? "Sometimes I have the oddest memories."

"Oh?" the nurse waited, but this time Jane was silent. "Naturally I don't have my references with me," the nurse said finally. "I'll bring them when I come back after my day off."

"Oh yes, of course." As she had feared, she had generated the antagonism and she had nothing to show for it. She was unreasonably convinced that when Janet Smith returned after her day off, she would have "forgotten" the references. Suddenly she said, "I have it! Dr. Stires said that my guardian recommended you. Do you know him? Howard Chalmers is his name."

"No, I don't," the woman said, her eyes more opaque than before. "Perhaps what Dr. Stires meant was that Mr. Chalmers took care of hiring me through the agency. I was simply told to report here. Perhaps that was because I have my own car and didn't mind working in the country. Most nurses won't accept a job so far from town."

"Yes, I suppose that's it. Well, I certainly am lucky to have found you so fast."

She *was* lucky. The nurse was more efficient at washing and dressing her and getting the room straightened than Zee had ever been. In addition, she was constantly finding extra jobs, like sorting out Jane's possessions. She was a treasure, except that Jane couldn't stand her. For one thing, she never left her alone. Unlike Zee, she had no interest in chatting with the kitchen help, or getting a ride into town with Kirk or watching television. She sat near Jane all day long, ready to get her anything she wanted. If there was no work to be done, she knitted or read, mostly "how-to" books, or listened to her transistor radio. She never left Jane's side for more than a few minutes at a time, even when she bathed. Jane felt strangled.

"Why don't you take a nap?" she suggested to the nurse on the third day of her attendance.

"I'm not tired. I never nap."

"Well—you know, I'm used to being on my own for hours at a time. You mustn't feel that you have to take care of me every minute."

"Do I disturb you?"

"No—of course not. I mean, I was thinking of *you*. I don't want you to feel tied down every—"

"I don't. This is what I'm paid to do."

Jane pretended to read but couldn't concentrate. The woman's personality seemed to her so overpowering that she could think of nothing else.

For the first time she began seeking out the company of the other patients. She made every effort to start a conversation with Marlene or Kirk, and even Bonnie's presence was strangely comforting. With odd intensity, she found herself counting the minutes until Miss Smith had her day off.

One afternoon, when the doctor came for his visit, she had difficulty conversing. In contrast to Miss Smith, who in the presence of the doctor abounded with interesting and amusing chitchat, she herself was almost completely dumb. She began to feel desperate when he rose to leave, and she wheeled herself along with him, wanting a word alone with him. But Miss Smith immediately rose and accompanied them. Through it all the doctor sensed nothing wrong.

She tried to reason herself out of the aversion. She had to relax and do what she had always done instead of try so hard to avoid the woman. She had a rosy-hued longing for the days before Miss Smith's arrival, as though they were a paradise lost. Even Gillian, Adeline, and the cook seemed like comforting old friends after a day in the company of Miss Smith. She began wheeling herself into the kitchen after dinner and trying to join their games of gin rummy. "You're acting funny," Gillian told her one night. "Are you all right?"

Like a child afraid of being punished, she found herself turning to look at the nurse's impassive face. "Of course I'm all right.

It's just that I'm getting better. Can you teach me the game?"

"It's not so good with three. I tell you what, though. Miss Smith, do you play bridge? We could teach Jane—"

"No, I don't," said Miss Smith. "I've never had time for cards. Shall we go back to the annex, Miss Wallcutt?"

Docilely Jane followed her, but she was raging within. She was bored with her restricted regime, tired of the unchanging routine, but afraid to protest. She was gradually growing fearful of everything, of asserting herself, of doing what she wanted, even of talking to the doctor. She was regressing, beginning to find it simpler to drift off again. It was like those first days she remembered, when it had been so pleasant to float, to allow the air currents to carry her away from the sights and sounds of reality.

Who was hiring whom, she kept telling herself. Suppose she fired Miss Smith?

The idea lay dormant for a while and then began to germinate. What would happen? Who would prevent it? Well, the doctor for one, Howard Chalmers for another, even Gillian because it would mean more work for her. Why, Jane, they would ask. What has she done wrong?

Sometimes she had a wild desire to write a note to someone, to anyone, calling for help as though she were a prisoner and could escape with assistance from the outside world. But her prison was wall-less and bar-less.

Friday evening she made a stab at independence. Waiting until after dinner, she stopped Miss Smith from wheeling her back to the annex by saying firmly, "I'm staying to watch television."

"Well—all right. One show, but I don't think you ought to stay up too late."

Trying to batten down her frustration, Jane said, "Why not? I feel fine."

"Well, for one thing you look quite tired, Miss Wallcutt. And for another—even Gillian remarked the other evening that you weren't quite yourself."

Wasn't quite herself? Then she remembered. "You're acting funny," Gillian had told her. How could she explain that it all stemmed from this smothering attention? The doctor, however, might argue that she had been "acting funny" for some time —imagining she had been shot at, hearing voices, suggesting that she was being threatened by a stranger in a Cadillac.

"I'll be watching for some time," she said evenly to Miss Smith. "You don't have to stay up if you don't care to."

"Who will help you undress and wash?"

"I'll ask Gillian for help."

"That wouldn't be quite fair, would it? She has enough to do. I'll stay with you," the nurse finished kindly.

"Oh, by the way, Miss Smith, which day do you prefer to have off—Sunday is fine with me."

"I'm not taking a day off. I made an arrangement to get paid for the seventh—"

Jane lifted a stricken face. She felt she was going to do something embarrassing. Like a rat in a maze, she thought. She kept darting frantically up dead ends. "I'd rather you took a day off," she said.

"Are you all right, Miss Wallcutt? You *do* look strange."

"I'm fine. Perfectly all right. I think everyone should have one day off a week."

"But I really don't mind. I prefer working."

"Well, Miss Smith, you see I'm the one employing you and I'd rather not pay for that seventh day." She felt her face flaming.

Kindly, Miss Smith said, "If it's the money you're worried about, Miss Wallcutt, I'll do without it. The fact is that I have no place to go on my day off. I just came here from Pennsylvania and I don't have an apartment."

Her head whirling, Jane began wheeling herself away. It made no sense, but she had a compelling need to remove herself from the vicinity of so much suction power. She would be swallowed alive if she didn't do something to save herself. Suppose she called someone, anyone, outside of the sanitarium? What would she say? Come get me, get rid of the nurse, help— No matter. She had to make a telephone call if only to prove that she *could* make one if she wanted to.

She found the telephone in the hall, high up and out of her reach. There was another one in the office. Of course, patients, as a rule, didn't go into the office—

"May I help you, Miss Wallcutt?"

She spun around. "Oh. Miss Smith. You startled me."

"I *am* sorry. Is there anything I can get you?"

"I want to make a telephone call," she said almost inaudibly.

"Let me make it for you. Whom do you want to call?"

"It's—it's—uh confidential. Could you hand me the phone?" God she was being ridiculous. Anyone in the house could listen in on a conversation out in the hall.

"You won't be able to reach the mouthpiece," Miss Smith pointed out.

She stared at the nurse stupidly. There was nothing but polite concern in the odd eyes. And, of course, she was right. "I guess I'll have to use the office telephone," she said, and making a wide circle around the nurse, who didn't move, she wheeled herself to the kitchen. Gillian, Adeline, and the cook were all there. "May I use the office telephone, Gillian?"

"The telephone! You never called anyone before. Who do you want to talk to?"

She couldn't get annoyed with Gillian. Everything she did stemmed from ignorance, not malice. "May I use it? Is there a telephone book in there?"

"Sure. I'll help you. To tell you the truth, I never saw you so jumpy before. Maybe you have spring fever." Gillian helped her along into the office, cleared a place on the cluttered desk, and gave her a local book. Some instinct made Jane turn. Miss Smith was standing in the doorway.

"No, Gillian—I want a New York book. I'd like to speak to

uh my fiancé." She felt that would be the safest choice. Instantly the familiar coyness erupted on Gillian's face. "I knew it was spring fever. Here it is. You take all the time you want. I'll put the call on your account. Come on, Miss Smith. You have to give a girl some privacy when she talks to her fiancé."

The two women went out. For a moment Jane hesitated, wondering if the hall telephone was on the same line as this one. Would Miss Smith take a chance on being caught listening in? She dismissed that and concentrated on whom to call, and what to say. Austin, Howard Chalmers, Gladys? Gladys had saved her—even if unintentionally—from the man in the Cadillac. She could trust her. Of course she didn't know her well, the way she was supposed to know Liz Dickinson, for instance, but she could invite her up again. At least it would mean talking to someone unconnected with the hospital.

She pushed the door shut and consulted the telephone book. There was a column and a half of Valentines. And only one Gladys, a Mrs. Gladys Valentine. But *her* Gladys wasn't married—at least she hadn't been wearing a ring. And if she lived with her parents, how could she tell which Valentine it was? As a matter of fact, she wasn't sure that Gladys lived in the city proper. The sense of her own helplessness was creeping up on her again. She could telephone the doctor and ask him for a list of numbers for everyone she knew. But even as she considered that possibility, her fingers were turning the pages. Bentley, Bernstein, Berol, Berque, Berquist. Fortunately it was not a common name.

What now? Ask for Gladys' number? Thank him for the gift? She had already sent him a note—at least she had written one and given it to Miss Smith. She would wish him a pleasant weekend in Washington. Her fingers trembling faintly, she dialed the operator who gave her the necessary code numbers.

"Mr. Berquist's answering service," a female voice said.

She let the air seep out of her lungs. Clearing her throat,

she asked, "I'd like to speak to Mr. Berquist. When will he be back?"

"He's out of town. Would you like to leave a message?"

Stupidly she said, "No, thank you," and hung up. She remained where she was for several minutes. She felt completely drained, as though she had been doing violent exercise. Without warning, the door opened. "Miss Wallcutt? Are you all right?"

"I'm fine. I'm not through yet, Miss Smith."

"I think you ought to go to bed. If you have difficulty sleeping, I'm sure the doctor could prescribe some sedative—"

"I don't want a sedative. I'm not tired and I don't have difficulty sleeping." The sharpness in her voice made Miss Smith lift one eyebrow. It was the word "sedative" that had brought it out. Suppose the nurse introduced a narcotic, a drug of some sort into her food that could—no, she wouldn't kill her. But she might give her something to produce hallucinations, bring on behavioral oddities.

"I have to make another call, Miss Smith. Would you mind shutting the door?" The intense eyes examined her for a moment and then the nurse said mildly, "Of course, Miss Wallcutt."

She went out into the hall but didn't quite shut the door and Jane wheeled herself over and shut it firmly. She knew, however, that anyone wanting to listen in could hear her. Nevertheless she riffled through the pages until she found Howard Chalmers.

Again a feminine voice said, "Chalmers residence."

"May I speak to Mr. Chalmers?"

"Who's calling please?" That meant he was home. She couldn't believe that she had actually contacted someone outside the hospital.

"Miss Wallcutt."

"Miss Wallcutt! How are you? I didn't recognize your voice, you sound so different. Are you feeling better?"

The voice was so warm, so genuinely concerned, she wanted

to reach out and hold the owner's hand. "I—I'm fine—but I don't —I lost my memory, you know—"

"Oh—I forgot. It's Nina, Miss Wallcutt. I know you for near eighteen years."

"Oh—perhaps I could—I would very much like to see you again, Nina," she said inanely, but the warmth of her own feelings must have touched the other woman. "Oh, we'll arrange it, Miss Wallcutt. I told Mr. Chalmers. You'd be no trouble for me. You come here any time you're sick of that hospital. Wait, Mr. Chalmers is right here."

His voice came on, pedantic, cordial, full of inquiries about her health. She went through the preliminaries, glancing at the door now and then. Finally he said, "Don't tell me you went through that thousand dollars right away and need more."

"No, of course not. I haven't spent any of it."

"That's not like my Janie."

"There isn't much to spend it on here."

"What does the doctor say? Will you be walking soon?"

"No—that is, he hasn't mentioned it, but I—" She wanted something from him, but she wasn't sure what. Perhaps it was what Nina had suggested—that she stay with him. If she had had a mother or father, that's what *they* would have suggested. They wouldn't keep her in a sanitarium for incurables indefinitely. Fighting tears of self-pity, she said, "I was wondering about the nurse—"

"Speak up, Jane. I can't hear you."

"I was wondering—where you got—that is, who recommended the nurse." Fearfully she glanced at the door.

"Why? Isn't she satisfactory?"

"Uh, yes, of course," she answered automatically. "Well, that is. What I mean—"

"Yes, my dear. What do you mean?"

"I can't—it's difficult speaking. I wonder if you could tell me —who recommended her?"

"*I* was the one who told Dr. Stires about her, my dear. He

called to tell me that your other nurse simply walked off— Did you say anything?"

"No—go on."

"And did I want to get someone else or leave it to him. Well, it just so happened I was going out to dinner that night and I knew there would be several people present who had needed the services of a nurse in the past—so I brought up the subject and got the name of this woman—Smith—and—"

"Do you know who gave you the name?"

"Well—let's see—it was a large group of people and I can't—"

"This person who recommended the nurse—did he or she give you the name of the agency?"

"No—let me see, who was it? Anyway, whoever it was, called the agency themselves and had her sent over. Why all the questions, Jane? What's wrong?"

"I—if I could see you—"

"Certainly, my dear. I have several things on this weekend, but if it's an emergency—"

"Oh no. It's not an emergency. But I'd love to see you. If it wouldn't be too much trouble—"

"Something must be wrong. You sounded quite content when I saw you last. Would you like me to cancel my appointments this weekend? They're not very important—a golf date, a dinner, brunch on Sunday—"

He waited for her to tell him it wasn't that important, and obediently, sadly, she told him what he wanted to hear.

Relieved, he said, "I'll see you next week, my dear. I'll call before I come. What would you like me to bring you?"

"Nothing. I just want to see you."

"How flattering you are to an old man, my dear. You're sure you don't want me to drop everything and come up this weekend?"

Of course she did. He must know she did. Dully she said, "No—come as soon as it's convenient."

She remained still again, staring at the cluttered desk. She didn't remember ever having felt so depressed. There was no one—no one in the entire world—on whom she could count. No one she could turn to and beg for help. What kind of person had she been to reach this state of abandonment? She rejected the thought. It was just that people always tended to forget the sick, the helpless, the feeble—but not if they had thirteen million dollars, surely?

Finally she pushed the door open and Miss Smith was right there, making no pretense of not having waited for her. There was no doubt that she had heard all the inquiries about the nurse.

16

By Sunday she felt that if she didn't do something or go somewhere all the nerves in her body would go haywire and she would start screaming. She had to remove herself from Miss Smith's vicinity.

"Please get my beige suit," she said. "I'm going to church."

"Church?" asked Miss Smith, astounded. "How?"

"Marlene invited me to her church. Of course she's a Catholic, but it doesn't matter. She's arranged the whole thing."

"But how will you get in and out of the car and then inside the—"

"She's asked someone to carry me."

"But Miss Wallcutt—you don't want—I mean, you can't ask strangers to *carry* you."

"Marlene said it would be all right."

"Marlene," Miss Smith said in a voice dripping with meaning, and then, to make sure Jane got the point, added, "Marlene is a *patient*."

And so was Jane, and as a consequence, neither one of them knew how to run her own life. Touching her head, she realized that it had been aching, on and off, for a week. She stared at the still-brownish lawn, and then at a watery sun trying to break through. She knew that if she argued she would either begin to shout or cry. "All right," she said and glanced at the nurse, as though expecting her to look triumphant, but there was no expression on the woman's face.

Someone knocked on the door, and when Jane called, "Come in," Marlene opened it. She stared at Jane in dismay. "You're not dressed, Miss Wallcutt!"

"Miss Smith thought it would be better if I didn't go," Jane said carefully.

Marlene stared at the nurse and then back at Jane. "Can't you make up your own mind?"

Something stirred in Jane. Whatever may have gone wrong with Marlene's mind, she still had character. "I'm going to church, Miss Smith," she said firmly. The nurse lifted her opaque eyes, and Jane knew that she would be made to pay for the spurt of independence.

"Who will carry you?" Miss Smith asked.

"It's all arranged for," Marlene said imperiously.

"You're sure he won't mind?"

"You may tip him."

"All right. I'm going." She waited for the nurse to help her, but instead the latter disappeared into her own room.

"Miss Smith!"

"I'll be right out, Miss Wallcutt."

When she finally emerged, she was all dressed for church herself.

Dismayed, Jane said, "There's no need for you to come."

"This uh—person may need help." Very slowly she helped Jane into her things while Marlene fidgeted.

It turned out that Miss Smith had been right. The whole process of carrying her back and forth to the car was embarrassing and attention-getting. At one point she dropped her purse, and at another point the nurse stumbled, almost letting her fall. In addition the service was long and boring. When they got back, she couldn't imagine why she had insisted.

The following week limped along interminably. Jane found herself waking just before dawn, dreading the long day ahead of her, and wondering why she bothered to go on living. At some point in the morning she would make up her mind that she would insist upon having Miss Smith fired, but when the doctor would arrive in the late afternoon, she would find it easier to do nothing than to go through the process of convincing him. Besides, Miss Smith never left them and always did all the talking. The only time she was alone was when Miss Smith went to the bathroom, and she only did that when Jane was on the bed instead of the wheel chair.

By the end of the following week she was staying up later and later in order not to have to go back to the annex with Miss Smith. With the rest of the dull-eyed patients, she would read or watch any television show. Bonnie would wander from person to person picking up scraps, Marlene would sit up stiffly and say almost nothing, Dick would smile, and Helen would continue to contemplate eternity.

On Friday evening Kirk began to play the piano and she listened with surprise. He played extremely well, she was sure, and it seemed incompatible, not with epilepsy but with the stock brokerage business. Nevertheless she didn't enjoy it. She was aware of a growing uneasiness as though the music had an unpleasant association for her. When he finished, she asked, "What was that?"

He turned slowly, as though lost in thought. Then, "Tchaikovsky's Concerto Number One. Why?"

"I don't know—I seem to remember—" She stopped as Miss Smith looked up. "Uh—you play very well. You must have been taking lessons for a long time."

"I started as a child."

"Did you ever do it professionally?"

"No."

She couldn't think of anything further to keep the conversation going and Kirk began to play again. Then, unexpectedly, Miss Smith got up and left the room. Since the nurse so rarely left her side, Jane stared after her suspiciously.

"What's wrong?"

She turned back, startled. Kirk was standing over her.

"I—uh—nothing. What makes you ask what's wrong?"

"Because I can tell something is."

She hesitated. The thought occurred to her that, although the doctor was completely unaware of her inner turmoil, two patients, Marlene and Kirk, were both trying to help her. Never-

theless she was afraid to say too much. "Well—I guess I'm getting
tired of this—this whole routine. It's boredom, that's all."

"Is that all?"

She glanced in the direction of the hall. "Well, not completely.
That is—I guess I miss Zee."

"You don't care for Miss Smith, do you?"

She wet her lips. "Not very much," she admitted.

"You ought to get away from here," he said abruptly. "Don't
you have someone who can take you for a while—although I'll
hate to see you go," he finished softly.

But she didn't hear the end of the sentence. She only heard
"You ought to get away from here." He was right. It was her only
salvation. With all her money there was no reason for her not
to have her own house and her own staff. The only problem
was getting someone to help her arrange it. But then, of course,
there would be no one around to protect her in case— It was the
same old circle.

Miss Smith returned with a glass of juice for herself and began to sip it, without asking Jane if she cared for any. Kirk
drifted out of the room and the two of them were alone with
Beth and Helen.

Jane picked up the newspaper and tried to pin her attention
to it. She half digested some information about a strike, city
politics, the war, and then, on the second page, a small item
caught her attention:

BODY OF WOMAN FOUND BY BOYS

Unreasoningly her heart began to thud as she read on.

The body, unclothed, had been found in a river in Virginia—

She stopped. Virginia? The story had no connection with what
she had been thinking. Why would "they" drive all the way to
Virginia to dispose of the body? So that it wouldn't be connected with anyone up here, that's why.

She read on. The woman, a negress, had been aged anywhere

from twenty-five to thirty-five and identification was going to be difficult because a warm spell had greatly increased the rate of bacterial decomposition. Distended with gases, the body had floated to the surface and been found by the boys, drifting head down. Fish, water rats, and the action of the water had removed a great deal of flesh from the body. Cause of death had not as yet been determined—

She stopped reading and was afraid she was going to be sick. The trembling in her hands made the newspaper rattle and she put it down carefully.

"What's the matter with you?"

"Nothing."

"You ought to be in bed. I think we'd better go back to the annex."

Her shoulders hunched, she allowed herself to be wheeled back.

17

By Saturday morning she still hadn't heard from Howard Chalmers. In addition, she had no idea whether or not Austin intended to visit her. When she went into the dining room for lunch, Miss Smith disappeared into the bathroom, and quickly Jane asked Gillian if there had been any calls for her. "Calls?" Gillian repeated absently, as she served the patients. "No, I don't think—wait, yes. You got one. From that what's-his-name, your guardian. I sent Adeline out—didn't she tell you?"

Stunned, Jane asked, "When was this? I didn't see Adeline."

"Maybe she couldn't find you." Nearly tripping over the dwarf's cane, she snapped, "Bonnie, move out of the way."

"Not find me! Where could I be? If I wasn't here I was in the annex. And if I wasn't in either place I was sitting outdoors between them."

"Well—if it was important, he'll call again."

"But I had to speak to him. Why didn't she tell me about it?"

"Don't get excited at *me*," Gillian said with asperity. "*I* had nothing to do with it. Dick, sit down."

Miss Smith emerged from the bathroom and Jane asked, "Did Adeline tell you there was a telephone call for me?"

"Telephone call?" the nurse repeated slowly, glancing at Gillian, as though wondering what she had said. "Oh—yes. You were lying in the sun, and I know how determined you are to get that suntan of yours, so I took it—"

"*You* took it!"

"Yes. I just explained. I hated to disturb—"

"Then why didn't you tell me he had called?"

"Didn't I? I thought I had. Anyway, it wasn't important. He asked how you were and if you still wanted to see him and I said it wasn't necessary—"

"You said *what?*" She noticed the rising hysteria in her own voice and tried to control it. "Wasn't that something for *me* to decide?" she continued more softly.

"He was obviously reluctant to make the trip. I know that you have a great deal of pride, Miss Wallcutt, and even if you are sick, you wouldn't want to be an imposition—"

"Imposition again!" Jane exploded. "Apparently I'm an imposition to nearly everyone. Perhaps what you really mean, Miss Smith, is that I'm an imposition to *you,* in which case—"

"Jane!" Gillian said in alarm. "You don't know what you're saying. Stay calm. Don't get excited. What'll we do if Miss Smith decides to leave?"

Jane turned to look at her, eyes blazing bitterly. But one glimpse of Gillian's face and the anger began to drain out. She couldn't blame Gillian for not wanting extra work. At the moment she had her hands full trying to get all the patients served. And she couldn't blame Howard Chalmers for being "reluctant" to give up an afternoon of golf in order to visit one of humanity's beached creatures. And most of all, she couldn't blame Austin for wanting to kill a relationship that had been dying anyway.

She couldn't eat. Despite Gillian's protests, she wheeled herself out into the hall. Instantly she heard the familiar footsteps behind her. She stopped and turned. "Miss Smith," she said calmly, "I'm not a small child. Nor an idiot. I can be trusted alone—for a short period anyway."

Irony was lost on the nurse. "Of course," she said soothingly, in a voice one might reserve for a child or an idiot. "I only wanted to see if you were all right. You looked so distraught—"

Jane wheeled herself away in the middle of the sentence. Miss Smith was like a sponge, lapping up all her energy, and she had to conserve it. She went straight to the office and found Adeline there, vacuuming the floor. "What are *you* doing here, Jane?" she asked, surprised.

"I'd like to make a call."

"Aren't you supposed to be eating lunch?"

"Adeline—if I ever get a call again, would you do me a favor?"

"Sure. What?"

"Never tell Miss Smith. Get me—no matter where I am."

"Oh—didn't you get to speak to Mr. Chalmers?"

"No—I know it wasn't your fault—could I make a call now?"

"I suppose so. Wait'll I finish. Did the doctor say it was all right?"

"Why not?"

"I don't know—anyway—I'm almost done." Adeline finally left and Jane found Austin's number and dialed it.

"Mr. Berquist's answering service."

She thought she would scream. Slowly she asked, "May I have Mr. Berquist's office number please?"

"I don't have that information."

"Do you know where I can reach him?"

"I'm sorry, I don't."

"Can you tell me if he's out of town?"

"He didn't let us know if he is."

"I'd like to leave a message. It's urgent. He's to call Miss Wallcutt."

When she had hung up, she went out into the hall again. She saw a movement around the door and was sure Miss Smith had been listening. Going down the ramp, she wheeled herself to a sunny spot and sat there, looking at nothing in particular. It was silly, she knew, but she had decided to remain within earshot of the telephone even if it meant not going back to the annex all day. Not that she had any clear idea of what she would say to him. "I'm afraid. Please visit me." Or, "I don't like my nurse. Get rid of her." What would his reaction be to that? "What's wrong with her?" "I don't know."

She watched Beth standing in the driveway, as though waiting for a visitor who would never come. Kirk, spreading lime on one of the fields, stopped to scoop up Hopeless, who had joined him. A car drove up to the gatekeeper's cottage across the road. Had it been rented? A reasonless alarm flared within her. I have to get over this feeling, she told herself, that everything is connected with me. It's sick.

By late afternoon she was feeling physically sick, too. She was getting hungry, but since she had voluntarily refused lunch, she didn't think it would be fair to ask the cook or Gillian to fix anything for her now. The nurse didn't come near her once and she wondered uneasily if she were sitting near the telephone, waiting to pounce. She had heard it ring several times, but no one had called her.

"You're going to be the color of an Indian if you don't look out." It was the doctor.

She glanced down at herself. "I think it looks good," she said listlessly.

"Why didn't you have lunch?"

"Who snitched?"

"It's your nurse's job to snitch."

"I didn't feel hungry—no, I was upset."

He looked around, found a chair and sat down. "Okay. Tell me."

"I—I was anxious to hear from Mr. Chalmers. And then— when he called, the nurse took it and never told me about it."

"Yes—she told me. She said you—uh—reacted rather strongly. Call him again."

She twiddled her fingers hopelessly. "So she told you I reacted strongly. It was smart of her to tell you first."

"Smart of her! What are you getting at now?"

"She—oh, it's so hard to explain. I wanted to ask Mr. Chalmers to visit me—"

"Call him now."

"He'll be out now. I know it. A day like this. And anyway, she said he didn't want to visit me—"

"What?"

"I mean—she made it sound so awful—as though I were a nuisance and he wouldn't want to waste a day coming here—"

"Jane, do you know what you're talking about? *I* don't."

She looked up at him, almost pleadingly, and he moved closer and took her hand. "Tell me slowly. What's the matter?"

"Please—" She swallowed and tried again. "It sounds unreasonable, I know. But I can't stand her. Could you please get rid of Miss Smith?"

He kept looking down at her hand and wouldn't meet her eyes. Finally he said, "Miss Smith said you might suggest that."

"Oh." She shut her eyes and little lights danced in the darkness. She knew she ought to eat something. "And since she told you first, it takes all the significance out of anything I might say."

"All right. Tell me what's wrong with her."

She had rehearsed this conversation so many times in her own mind she knew exactly what he would say. "Our personalities clash. She—she makes my skin crawl. She never leaves me alone."

"That's what a nurse is for."

"Do you realize this is the first time she's allowed us to speak together since she arrived? And that's only because I finally told her to keep away."

"You told her that?"

"Yes. Didn't she inform you? She won't take a day off. She's always—"

"I should think that a nurse who won't take a day off is a treasure."

"Oh God, oh God—"

"Take it easy. Suppose you don't like the next nurse. Then what do we do?"

"I liked Zee."

"Zee was here when you came out of— She was part of the only world you knew. Like a baby and its mother. It doesn't question its mother. But Miss Smith is a new experience."

"She watches every move I make. She listened when I tried to call Austin before."

"You called Austin? How do you know she listened?"

"I saw her dress disappear around the doorway as I came out of the room."

"Are you sure? Your eyes—"

"Oh—what's the use. Doctor—" She thought of asking him to tell the police about the body found in the water in Virginia, but she changed her mind.

"What?"

"Nothing."

"Would you like something to eat?"

She looked into his kind eyes and was afraid that her own ever-ready tears might spill out. "Yes." She tried to laugh but it sounded like a sob. "I'm starved."

"I'll send Adeline out."

He went off and in a short time Adeline arrived with a cheese sandwich, milk, and an apple. Kirk passed by and invited her to the greenhouse and Marlene invited her to the birdhouse, but she refused them both, afraid to leave her post. The food and the attention cheered her up, however, and she felt less alone. There *were* people who cared. Even if they were people like Kirk and Marlene.

The next time the telephone rang, she heard Gillian calling her. She almost overturned the wheel chair in her hurry to get indoors. Miss Smith appeared from one of the rooms to help her and she was terrified that the nurse would find some way to stop her. "I'm coming," she called several times.

"You'll hurt yourself, Miss Wallcutt," the nurse said solicitously. "And don't shout so. You're upsetting the other patients."

The "other" patients. She moved more slowly, chilled at the reminder that she was akin to Bonnie, for instance. The nurse wheeled her into the office and she said, "Thank you," and waited. When Miss Smith left, she pushed the door shut.

"Hello?"

"Jane? It's Austin."

The relief was so great she lost her breath completely.

"Jane? Are you still there?"

"Yes—I uh was hurrying."

"What's wrong? You said it was urgent."

Until this moment it had seemed to her that all her troubles would be over the moment she heard his voice, but now she didn't know what to say. She was like a dog in agony, unable to tell its master what was wrong.

"Austin—"

"Well?"

"I feel a little silly—I mean saying it was urgent. I just, well —I hadn't heard from you in two weeks—and it was so dull around here—and the new nurse—" All her efforts to sound light, fell flat. "I just can't stand the nurse."

"Why?"

"Oh—it's hard to explain. She *clings*—like uh molasses—she's so uh—depressing—she—"

"I see." His voice was neutral.

He was like the doctor. She couldn't reach him. There was no way out. Everywhere she turned she was blocked. Anything she said would make it worse.

"Oh well—what I really wanted to say was thank you for the present. I love it. I also like Gladys Valentine. I must get your, I mean I must get her address—oh, by the way, what made you think I might need a St. Christopher medal?"

"*I* didn't think you needed it. But *you* seemed to think you did."

"Oh well—thank you anyway. And uh—I hate to impose but I—"

"You hate to *what?*"

"I said, well, I said I hate to impose but—"

"Have you been listening to soap operas lately?"

"Well, everyone around here seems to think I'm such a burden. The nurse said it was an imposition to invite Howard Chalmers up here, and everyone thought it was too big a deal to take me to church, and Gillian is afraid I'll overwork her if the nurse leaves—"

"What in God's name is wrong with you?"

"Oh—nothing—it's just—I mean I'm bored, that's all. Will you —that is, were you planning on visiting me this weekend?"

"Well, no, not this weekend. The Greer case is coming up— what did you say?"

"You—you absolutely can't—"

"Well, do you want me to be a success or don't you? I was in the office this morning and I really ought to go over all this paper work. What's wrong?"

"Oh—what a fool I am—I didn't mean to—" She was crying, and she was afraid he would think she was doing it deliberately, asking for pity. "I'm sorry. I know you think I'm neurotic . . . I'll be all right in a minute . . ."

"Listen," he said, his voice suddenly businesslike. "Can you wait until next week? I'll pick you up Saturday as soon as I can get away, and you can stay at my mother's house for a while. I don't know what's wrong, but maybe you can use a change."

"Oh—" She nearly lost her breath and then the sobs became worse. "I couldn't impose on your mother—"

"Don't be an ass. Get yourself packed—I mean tell your nurse to pack—and tell her she's coming too—"

"My nurse? She'll be coming?"

"Well—you need someone, don't you? Besides I want to get a look at her. If I see anything wrong, we'll get rid of her. I'll pick you both up at, oh, say, early afternoon. Is that all right? Or do you still want me to come today?"

"I—no, I couldn't be ready—that is, I can stand it another week if—if—you're sure you'll come next week?"

"Unless I'm killed in an earthquake, but as there aren't many earthquakes in these parts—"

"Suppose your mother—"

"You know my mother— Oh, I forgot. You don't. She'll be delighted. She's suggested it several times but I wasn't sure you were ready."

"I—Austin, you're sure nothing will go wrong?"

"I never saw you like—" He stopped. "Yes, I'm sure."

She couldn't bear breaking the connection. Desperate for a topic, she asked, "Did you get my letter?"

"What letter?"

Another confirmation of her fears. Trying to keep her voice calm, she said, "I sent you a thank you note for the medal. I gave it to Miss Smith to mail."

There was a pause. "Well," he said finally, "you know those small post offices. Anyway, what's the point? I mean, in not mailing it? She knew you could contact me on the phone."

"Well—but, well it *was* rather difficult to get you. I mean you're not home very much."

"Why don't you ask her if she mailed it?"

"No—that is, I—if she did *not* mail it, she wouldn't admit it, would she?"

"Well—I'll see you next week."

She knew that once he had hung up, once the thread was broken, the noxious fears would seep up around her again. "I—uh, Austin?"

"Yes?"

But she couldn't think of anything else. "Thank you."

Again there was a pause. Then, somewhat sarcastically, "You're welcome." She couldn't understand the tone of his voice. It wasn't antipathy. Dissatisfaction? No, distrust was more like it. Distrust of what?

She wheeled herself out into the hall and found Miss Smith waiting for her.

"I thought perhaps you might need me to get ready for dinner."

She hadn't wanted to tell the nurse until the last moment, for fear that she might try to stop her. But in all probability she knew already.

"Miss Smith," she said, trying to keep her voice neutral, "I've been invited to visit my fiancé's mother's house next Saturday."

"For how long?"

"I—I really don't know. I'll—I'll have to get some clothing

ready. We'd better look over my things. I want some skirts shortened and I want you to get a hairdresser to come up here. Of
course, if *you* would prefer not to go . . ."

"I'd be delighted, Miss Wallcutt. I think a change of scene
would suit both of us."

Jane glanced at her quickly. Uneasily she realized that the
nurse didn't seem to be against the idea. She was thinking.

18

Either Mrs. Berquist had planned a party for her, or it was the kind of house where people dropped in. When they turned up the macadam driveway, she saw seven or eight cars parked in front.

The house was a large old yellow brick surrounded by a poor lawn and thick old trees. On one side someone had prepared a large bed for flowers.

She felt nervous as Austin picked her up and went to the door. Behind them came Miss Smith, carrying two suitcases. A young girl who was wearing an ordinary house dress instead of a uniform opened the door. She was as uneasy as Jane as she said, "Hello, Mr. Austin. They're all in the back." She spoke with a Swedish accent.

Austin put Jane on a bench in the entrance hall for a moment, and she examined the stone floor, the curving staircase, and the largish living room beyond as he showed Miss Smith the downstairs bedroom.

"Well?" he asked, when he returned.

Misunderstanding, she said, "It's lovely."

"What I mean is, does it strike a chord? Do you remember it?"

"Where can I find the wheel chair Mrs. Berquist rented?" Miss Smith asked.

"I don't— Ask Karen."

"No," Jane said. "I don't remember. I'm sorry."

He picked her up again and carried her through the living room. It was crammed with heavy furniture, portraits, books and musical instruments. It occurred to her that, although Austin's family seemed to be well off, they weren't nearly as rich as she was.

Outdoors, past the French windows, there was a stone terrace with chaises, chairs, and tables. A number of people, casually dressed in a wild array of cottons, although it was only April, were sitting around drinking. She felt like Rip Van Winkle. She had asked Miss Smith to have the green wool dress and coat taken in and shortened, but the nurse had been unable to find a dressmaker. She had also been unsuccessful in finding a hairdresser. Jane's long, straight hair, however, wasn't nearly as out of place as the urban outfit.

"Janie! How marvelous you look. What a lovely tan. I'm so glad you're here at last." As Austin put her down, one of the women, hands outstretched, bent and kissed her. "I told that son of mine I wanted to visit you, but he insisted that you see me in my natural setting the first time. He wanted to jog your memory." She laughed. "Somehow it doesn't look jogged."

"No—I'm sorry. I don't remember—"

"And you're Miss Smith," Mrs. Berquist went on, shaking the nurse's hand.

Austin's mother wasn't what Jane had expected—a "well preserved"-looking woman with a neat figure and gray hair. The gray hair was there, but otherwise she was round and middle-aged. Her face had been pretty once, but she had done nothing to keep it that way. Oddest of all, she was wearing a long, unflattering but comfortable-looking muumuu. His father, however, was more in keeping with her preconceived picture of a tall, distinguished-looking man. He spoke pedantically, like Howard Chalmers. "It's very nice to see you, Jane. How does it feel to be back in the world?"

"Lovely. Absolutely lovely."

When she had seen the cars, she had been afraid she would have to meet a great many strangers, but Mrs. Berquist had invited the Dickinsons, Gladys Valentine, and Howard Chalmers, as well as a few people she didn't remember. There was Austin's sister, whose existence she hadn't suspected, as well as the latter's husband, and a few old friends of the Berquists.

Mr. Berquist offered her a martini, but it was warm in the late afternoon sun, and she saw something in a tall frosted glass. "I wonder—could I have one of those?"

He seemed surprised, but he went to get her one.

"If you'd like to change, Miss Smith," Mrs. Berquist said pleasantly, "Karen will show you to your room."

Miss Smith, who had seated herself behind Jane, not quite a guest and not quite a servant, said, "I'm fine, Mrs. Berquist. I put on a fresh uniform before we left."

Evidently Austin had told his mother about Jane's aversion to her nurse. Firmly Mrs. Berquist said, "Then perhaps you'd like to get Miss Wallcutt's clothing unpacked."

The nurse looked up, her strange opaque eyes on Mrs. Berquist. Around them everyone was chatting, but the two women seemed to be set apart from the others. Almost as though she were afraid that her hostess would be bewitched in some manner, Jane broke the deadlock. "Uh, Miss Smith—the weather is so unusually warm, I'm going to need something lighter. Would you check and see if any of the silks or cottons need ironing?"

The eyes turned on her, and she felt herself flinching. It was like pulling a lion's tail to distract his attention from another victim. She would be made to pay for this too, the way the nurse had already punished her by not having her clothing shortened or her hair done. "Certainly, Miss Wallcutt."

"Your drink, Jane." It was Austin.

"Oh—I'm sorry—I didn't see—"

"You say, 'I'm sorry,' once more and I'll pop you."

"Oh, I'm so—I mean—" She began to laugh. "This drink is heavenly. What is it?"

"Planter's punch." He was watching her with odd intentness, and confused, she turned away and began listening to the conversations around her.

"The talk of a plot was utter nonsense," her guardian was saying. "It was just one crackpot."

"Of course you're right," Austin's brother-in-law, Wilson,

agreed. "A lot of people are killed senselessly by people who should be in hospitals."

Liz Dickinson disagreed. "You're ignoring a great many things which weren't explained. When some people have a theory, they discard all the facts which tend to refute it."

Listening to them, Jane thought how alike their voices sounded, deep, clipped, well enunciated. She shut her eyes in order to see if she could tell which one was talking. Only Gladys Valentine sounded different. "How have you been getting along since I saw you last?" Gladys was asking her.

"Fine—well, not really."

"No? Why not?"

"I must be one of those chronic malcontents who's never satisfied. Incidentally, I tried to call you once but couldn't find your name in the book."

"Was there something in particular you wanted to tell me?"

"Well—no. I just wanted to ask you to visit me."

"Tell me why you're not satisfied. What's bothering you?"

It struck her as odd that Gladys didn't offer to give her the telephone number. Just then Austin returned with a segmented dish containing olives, radishes, and a creamy mixture on toast rounds. She was reluctant to discuss it with him around, but Gladys persisted. "What was your problem?"

"Her nurse," Austin said, glancing at Gladys as though some private understanding existed between them. Suddenly Jane wondered if Gladys was a friend of Austin's rather than of hers. A person without a memory could be told anything. She tried to reassess Gladys—she was homely, of course, but she had a warm personality and intelligence, and possibly other hidden qualities. The thought was so upsetting, she took a huge drink to drown it.

"—seems normal enough to me," Austin was saying. "Maybe she *is* a little annoying—I mean about sticking around just now —but all of those so called 'practical' nurses tend to be peculiar."

"You can say that again." It was Austin's sister, Patty. "I had a horror when I came home from the hospital after having Corky.

Everyone told me it was just postnatal nerves, but I felt that if I didn't get the creature out of the house, I would start screaming. She never left me alone. Even when Wilson came home in the evening."

"The gun dropped by the South American didn't have his fingerprints on it," Liz was saying. "Now—he was shot immediately by that policeman. How could he have wiped off his fingerprints?"

"Nonsense." It was a man Jane didn't know. "At a time of crisis, very few people know exactly what's happening. Anyone could have picked up the gun before the policeman got to it."

"Then why weren't there smudged prints? But it was clean."

"Suppose someone with gloves picked it up—a woman who happened to be standing by? Or suppose the policeman picked it up exactly where the assassin held it? He could have covered the killer's prints. After all, how many ways are there to hold a gun?"

"What a policeman!"

"Think of the situation. The governor shot, thousands of people milling around—he might have had to grab the gun just to keep it from getting lost underfoot."

The drink was stronger than it tasted. She felt strangely light-headed. Turning to Austin, she said, "Talking about plots—"

His face seemed to grow shadowed as though someone had passed a tinted glass over it.

"Oh—I know you're tired of my—uh—sessions—I mean, obsessions—but there's something I have to talk to you about—have they found Zee yet?"

"Zee?"

"My former nurse."

"Oh. I haven't heard anything."

"You mean no one's checked or— No, why should you—"

"What did you mean—talking of plots?" It was Gladys.

"Oh—my first nurse left me, you know—and well, I—I read a

story in the newspaper about a woman's body being found—a Negress, about Zee's age—and well—I guess I'm morbid."

"Where did all this happen?" Austin asked.

"Well, that's the catch." She took another swallow of the drink. "But if I were hiding a body, I'd do the same thing. I'd take it as far from the scene of the crime as possible. It was fished up in Virginia."

"Virginia!"

"It's possible. I wish—I want to call Zee's sister and check—"

"I'm sure the police are doing whatever is necessary."

"Yes—but, you might mention the body in Virginia. There might be some way to identify it. The article said it was uh—decomposed."

"Well, then, it couldn't be Zee. She didn't disappear long enough ago to be decomposed."

Unexpectedly Gladys said, "You're wrong there, you know."

He looked at her.

"It depends upon the conditions," she went on. "I heard of one case in which a man was submerged in water for two weeks in June off Long Island, and he was only a skeleton when they found him."

A woman's figure came around the side of the house, and rising, Mrs. Berquist said, "Ellis! How nice!"

"I saw all those cars," the newcomer said, "and I was thirsty, so I decided to invite myself in for a drink."

"You can invite yourself to more than that. Stay for dinner. Come and meet everyone." Mrs. Berquist led the newcomer to Jane. Dressed in crisp, clean-looking golfing clothes, the woman called Ellis was small, slim, and had dark hair in a net, and sharp, ferretlike features. Her eyes seemed to be permanently narrowed, as though constantly appraising the world. "I want you to meet Ellis Hamden. Jane Wallcutt."

Jane put down her drink and tried to see the woman more clearly. "I know Mrs. Hamden," she said without warning.

"What?" Mrs. Berquist stared at her, but the other woman

didn't appear to have heard. She had moved on to the others and someone asked her how she had done.

"Eighty-nine. Remember the dog leg on the sixth? I took the putter, but instead of going back, I tried to go forward—"

Puzzled, Jane was saying, "I guess I must have seen her somewhere since the accident."

"—can't get the wedge down to the ball. It's better to use a three iron."

"Maybe she reminded me of someone," Jane went on. Mrs. Berquist, Austin, and Gladys were all staring at her. "Stop looking at me like that."

Irritably Austin said, "Of all the people here, Ellis Hamden is the last one I'd expect you to remember. She's just some divorcée Mother met at the club."

"Well—I can't help it. I get these flashes of recognition sometimes when I see a certain face or, or—a color, or even when I catch a certain odor—"

"She *does* have an odor," Austin admitted, "but she was just playing golf."

"You look a lot better than you did the last time I saw you." It was Howard Chalmers. Sitting down beside her, he went on, "I wanted to come up and visit you again, my dear, but your nurse made me feel that you preferred not to have an old man around."

"It's not true! I wanted to see you very badly. I can't tell you—I was—I was so depressed last week—"

"You should have called."

"Well, I tried—but anyway—I'm so glad to be here with you all."

"You must come to my apartment when you're tired of the hospitality around here." He smiled at Austin. "Or maybe I can rent a little place. Nina said she'd be glad to take care of you."

"Oh, how nice you all are. How I wish I didn't have to be 'taken care of.'"

"Only people with mental aberrations see plots everywhere.

One crackpot took a shot at the governor and that was all there was to it."

She was definitely beginning to feel dizzy. The conversations around her surged and ebbed like the ocean, lifting her and dropping her. The talk of guns fused with handicaps and woods, and in one corner of the terrace, bridge scores melted into a discussion of children. A large dog came bounding out on the lawn, sniffing at everyone. Jane reached down and patted him, and instantly he settled beside her, nuzzling her hand with his nose. She had a sudden longing for Hopeless.

"Are you tired?"

Her eyes had closed without her knowing it. Opening them, she saw Austin watching her. "No, I'm fine."

"Perhaps you'd like to lie down before dinner."

The thought of going indoors to Miss Smith deterred her. "No—I can relax here."

"Look," Mrs. Berquist was saying. "Schubert remembers Jane."

Lazily Austin drawled, "He'd go to a cross-eyed beggar with three feet if he were petted."

"Oh how flattering you are." It was Ellis Hamden.

Austin looked at her uncomprehendingly for a moment, and then he grinned. "Jane *does* have a problem with her eyes—don't you, pet?"

It was the first endearing term she remembered hearing him use, and she was just turning to him when her attention was distracted by two children who arrived several hundred yards behind the dog.

"Jane, these are Patty's children—and Wilson's," Mrs. Berquist added, as an afterthought.

She saw a boy of about four and a girl of about seven. They were dressed in faded Levi's and loose shirts, and both were barefooted. Unself-consciously, they approached the group on the terrace and Mrs. Berquist said, "You'd better get washed—or no dinner."

Paying no attention, as though they were accustomed to ignoring her, they stared at Jane's legs. Evidently they had been warned.

"You got legs," the little boy said in surprise. "Why can't you walk?"

In a loud clear voice the girl said, "It's not polite to discuss things like that." The guests tittered, but nervously.

"I was hurt in an accident."

"Wassanaccident?" the little boy asked.

"Come here. I'll tell you." He came without hesitation, and she lifted him on to her lap.

"Here we go." Liz laughed. "Jane the Mother."

"You'll get filthy," Mrs. Berquist sighed. "How did you get all that dirt on you, Corky?"

"I'm only a child," he said plaintively and everyone laughed again, this time more easily. He reached up to grab Jane's St. Christopher medal, and accidentally his cheek brushed hers.

Suddenly, and without warning, she burst into sobs.

19

She was clutching the child uncontrollably, and the little boy, alarmed, struggled to free himself. But she couldn't let go, and her sobs broke into the calm garden like something unspeakable released from the woodwork.

Getting up quickly, Austin tried to loosen her hold, while his sister clucked nervously, "Corky, stop that. Stop acting so silly," although all Corky was doing was trying to get down. Everyone else looked embarrassed. Finally Austin disengaged the boy, and his mother hustled him off. Then, without warning, Austin lifted Jane in his arms and carried her inside the house.

It was cool and dark after the terrace, and he waited a moment for his eyes to become adjusted to the gloom. "Do you want to go to your room or to the study?" he asked.

She had controlled the sobs, but she couldn't answer. It was all over now. They would take her back to the hospital and leave her there with Miss Smith. She couldn't be counted on for civilized behavior. After waiting so long for this, she had ruined everything.

Austin carried her into her own room, and Miss Smith, unpacking, glanced up in surprise. She stared at Jane for a moment and then asked, "Were you crying, Miss Wallcutt?"

"Miss Smith," Austin said crisply, "would you excuse us?"

She raised her eyebrows. "I was sent in here to unpack, and now—"

"I'd like to talk to Miss Wallcutt alone."

She hesitated a moment and then walked out, leaving the door open. Austin kicked it shut and put Jane on the bed, sweeping a pile of clothing on to an armchair. He sat down beside her and waited until he was sure she had calmed down. Then, "Do you want a glass of water?"

She shook her head drearily. He glanced around, saw her purse, took out a handkerchief and handed it to her. She dried her eyes and blew her nose. Finally he said, "All right. What happened?"

She looked at him, thinking how inaccessible he was. *Mens sana in corpore sano,* while she—

"I don't know," she said tiredly. "It sounds impossible, but I really don't know."

He was silent for a while, and then he let his breath out in a long sigh.

"What a fool I made of myself," she went on. "You must be so embarrassed. And after I practically forced you to bring me here— I don't know how to apologize. You can take me back tomorrow if you like—"

"How can you not know? Think, damn it. Make your mind work."

Sadly she said, "You're convinced it's all a matter of will, aren't you? You sound like a football coach giving the team a pep talk."

"For God's sake, Jane, if *you* won't help yourself, what can the rest of us do?"

"Nothing," she whispered. "I'm hopeless."

"Oh shut up," he snapped. "And stop feeling so sorry for yourself."

She looked down at her hands. Stop feeling so sorry for yourself. Why was self-pity always considered the lowest form of behavior? "It was probably the drink," she said, her voice hardening. "I'm not used to liquor."

"It *had* to be more than that."

"Well, he was the first child I've held since— There were children in the fire—"

He was silent, so silent, she tried to see his expression, but the room was too dark. She would have asked him to put on the light except that she was sure that her skin was spotted, her eyes red-rimmed, and her hair a mess. Why hadn't she remained quietly where she was and not annoyed anyone? She was no better off here than she had been in the hospital. No, she was worse off. She wasn't slipping backward, she felt, but going forward, drawn toward some inevitable catastrophe. This visit had brought her closer to whatever it was.

"Listen—"

"Yes?" she asked. She felt he was about to say something important and she had to strain her mind to understand.

"Tell me everything again."

"What do you mean?"

"You know—"

"You mean everything I remember?"

"No—that is, unless it's something new. I mean about those uh—threats—your suspicions—"

"Oh." She turned away toward the window. "Why? You'll just consider me paranoid."

"Miss Wallcutt," the nurse said, opening the door without knocking, "dinner is ready. Mrs. Berquist wanted to know if you—"

"Tell Mrs. Berquist to start without us," Austin snapped. "And please don't come in without knocking, Miss Smith."

Slowly the blood rose to her face. She stared at him unbelievingly. "Mr. Berquist, I'm not accustomed—"

"A patient is entitled to privacy, Miss Smith."

"I've never been spoken to in this manner in my whole life."

"Miss Wallcutt has never been treated in this manner in her whole life. She is a normal adult, in spite of her inability to walk. And you've been treating her like a child. It's inexcusable."

Uneasily Jane wondered what would happen if she had to go back to the sanitarium with Miss Smith. It would be better to fire her immediately. But in that case, Mrs. Berquist would have an invalid on her hands—

"I didn't realize I was treating her like a child," Miss Smith said, and her voice was emotionless again. It was obvious she had decided not to take offense. The thought chilled Jane more than if she had walked out in a huff. Miss Smith was determined not to be fired. Turning quietly, she went out, and this time she shut the door behind her.

When she was gone, Austin said, "All right. Tell me about your uh—the threats against your life."

"I don't think you should have spoken to her like that."

"You're afraid of her. Why?"

"I told you—I don't know. There's something about her—"

"All right. Tell me everything."

She went through it slowly, trying to act matter-of-fact and unhysterical, but she must have played it down too much, because when she was through he said, puzzled, "You sound so—casual. As though—well, as though you were telling me about a dream."

She shut her eyes. "If I act emotional, everyone says I'm sick. If I act calm, everyone says it couldn't have happened. I can't win."

When she opened her eyes, she saw that he was grinning. "You sure do have it tough," he said unsympathetically. Then, "What made you think you knew Ellis Hamden?"

"I—I'm not sure anymore."

Oddly, he didn't pursue it but asked instead, "Did you like her or dislike her?"

She hesitated, wondering what the question meant. Then automatically she started to say, "How could I dislike someone I just me—" but she stopped. She had to be honest, no matter how unbalanced it made her appear. "I hated her."

Matter-of-factly he said, "I'm not overly fond of her myself."

"Why?"

"I don't know."

"See?" she said triumphantly. "It's possible to have an inex-plicable feeling."

"Well—actually I do know. She's cold and unemotional. She's too noncommittal. No one could have so few opinions."

No one could have so few opinions. Jane listened intently,

waiting for something, she wasn't sure what. A clue, a key . . .
"Go on," she prompted.

"That's all."

"Oh," she said, disappointed. She had been on the verge of
pouncing, and her prey had eluded her again.

He stood up. "Let's go down to dinner."

"Oh—I can't—please—"

"For Pete's sake—you can't hide forever."

"It would be too embarrassing. I made such a fool of myself.
And poor little Corky. I terrified him."

"He's forgotten it already. And stop hiding behind a little boy.
Listen—are you going to try to behave like a mature woman
and get out of this—whatever it is you're stuck in, or are you
going to be an ostrich for the rest of your life?"

Stalling, she asked, "What's wrong with an ostrich?"

"Well, they look like hell with their heads in the sand and
their rears sticking up like that."

"I'll start being mature tomorrow. I look awful—"

"You'll start now. You look fine. Wash your face and do whatever girls do and let's get going."

She wanted to stamp her feet and shout with frustration, but
she was afraid that if she gave in to that whim, she might never
be given another chance. Something was happening to Austin.
He wasn't quite as unreachable as he had been, but he was still
teetering, as though on the brink of a decision, and if she did
the wrong thing, he might end up on the other side of the fence.

As though the words were forced from her with pincers, she
said, "All right. I'll go down. Call Miss Smith, please."

She shut her eyes tiredly, afraid of being alone with the nurse,
afraid of going downstairs, afraid of his displeasure.

And then something incredible was happening. It was so unexpected that, at first, the sensation was unrecognizable. She had
no intimation of it until she smelled the faint mixture of tobacco
and alcohol, and she felt something strange on her lips. His
arms encircled her, lifting her off the pillow and against his

chest. He was rough at first, as though he wanted to hurt her, but gradually the contact worked a chemical change within him, and the pressure relaxed. She found her lips parting as his hand moved, and it was as though a dam had broken and a dozen unforeseen sensations coursed through her. Fear drained away as if a wound had been opened, and the vacuum was filled with a new and yet familiar combination of pain and sweetness. A force she couldn't remember made her entwine her arms, almost against her will, around his neck. A curtain in her mind twitched, and lost in a torrent that flooded her mind she whispered, "George. George."

20

For a moment nothing much happened. He swallowed and moved his lips to her throat. And then, as though the words had just caught up with his brain, he jerked back and dropped her on the pillows.

"What did you say?" he asked incredulously.

She blinked and tried to clear her mind. "Wh-when?"

"What do you mean when?" he asked furiously. "Just now, damn it."

"I didn't say anything."

He stood up and ran a hand back over his hair. His brows contracting with disbelief, he said, "Are you serious?"

"I don't—I really don't—"

"You called me George."

"George," she repeated, puzzled. "You're sure?"

"My God!" He turned around, went to the window, changed his mind, and banged the wall switch savagely, flooding the room with light. He stared at the messy bed and her ravaged face, and sat down again.

Gradually the anger dried up. A new expression seemed to be fighting to slip over his face, but he wasn't ready for it. He frowned, bit his lip, and stared at her.

"You have lipstick on your mouth," she said.

He kept staring at her as though he was having difficulty with his hearing. Then he put his hand to his mouth and, unexpectedly, grinned. "Where else should it be?" He stood again. "Let's have dinner."

"Do you know where that rented wheel chair is? I hate to make you carry me everywhere."

"Is it that painful?" He stood over her, his hands in his pockets and his eyes intent.

She turned away. "I have to wash. It will only take a minute. Would you call Miss Smith?"

"Who needs her?" He lifted her in his arms and her face brushed his, but he didn't kiss her. Putting her down on the closed toilet seat, he asked, "Can you manage if I leave you?"

"Oh yes. I hold on to the wall and things. The dress I want is that long cotton thing—the one with flowers."

She heard him rummaging in the closet as she splashed water on her face. Holding on to the sink with both hands, she lifted herself gingerly and looked into the mirror. The blotches had faded. She washed hurriedly, put on lipstick, combed her hair and called out that she was ready. He lifted her again and placed her on the bed. The dress was there. "What else?"

"The sandals. Thank you."

"Sure you can manage without me?"

"Perfectly sure."

"I'll be in the hall."

He left the door open and she heard him whistling an odd tune. She pulled off the wool dress and her stockings and shoes, and got into the flowered thing which appeared to be a kind of hostess outfit. "I'm ready."

"Very pretty," he said, lifting her. "When did you get it? Damn, I keep forgetting."

He held her gingerly as though afraid that if he got too close, she might have a lapse and call him by another name again.

"What were you whistling?" she asked, to mask her own nervousness. She could hear their voices coming from the other room.

"What? Oh. I can't get the blasted thing out of my mind. It's from the play we saw—you know."

"What are the words?"

"Well—are you sure you want to hear?"

"Yes. Why not?"

He began to sing. " 'Oh it's all right to lie, but not in front of the children. It's all right to die, but not in front of the children. Make a pass—' "

"What a terrible song."

"Oh—well, it seemed all right then—I mean, well, afterwards, it seemed sort of horrible—"

They were in the living room now and she could see all the faces, blurred ovals, turn in their direction. Not knowing whether it would be better to ignore her own behavior or apologize for it, she decided it would be acting less like an ostrich if she said immediately, "I'm sorry for my outburst. I guess I'm going to be unpredictable until I get my memory back."

"Remember how I kept bursting into tears after Corky was born?" Patty said to her husband, and the subject was dropped. They all went into the dining room and Liz told Jane how lovely she looked, after which she launched into a discussion of a garden tour. The children were nowhere to be seen. The conversation came to Jane as though through a screen and she realized that she had had too much to drink. She caught snatches of gossip, a discussion about a book, references to social events. While she ate, she wondered if, because one of her faculties was gone, another had sharpened. She had heard of blindness leading to acuteness of hearing, but never of amnesia leading to—what? She had no name for it.

She felt more sensitive to influences that she might not have noticed once. There was an evanescence in the room that seemed to be engulfing her. Her sharpened awareness kept insisting that she take particular notice of everything that was happening, but all she could see was a group of people chatting. On her left, Mr. Berquist was discussing stock fluctuations with a woman she didn't know, and on her right, Austin's brother-in-law was trying to interest her in a variety of subjects ranging from politics to music. Austin was at his mother's end of the table, talking to Liz, and Gladys was laughing at a remark of a man Jane didn't know. Evidently Miss Smith was in the kitchen with the children. The only one not saying anything was Ellis Hamden. Carefully Jane avoided looking at her. The air seemed filled with electrical currents.

It wasn't until Monday morning that Jane put a tag to the impressions she had had during the dinner party: extrasensory perception (the electrical currents having been brain waves instead of the more usual kind), but even as she thought it, she called herself an ass.

What triggered the thought was the telephone call. It came immediately after breakfast. Austin and his father had both left for work, the weekend guests had departed, and only Jane, Mrs. Berquist, Miss Smith, and the maid were in the house.

Confirming her fears, Mrs. Berquist came into the room and said, "Oh Jane—Ellis Hamden just called."

Although until then she hadn't known what she was waiting for, the name made her sure. This was it. "Yes?" she said carefully, not looking at the nurse.

"Isn't it nice of her?" Mrs. Berquist went on warmly. "The club's having a fashion lunch today, and it just occurred to her that it might break up the week for you. She invited you to go."

"How would I get there?"

"It's less than half a mile down the road. She invited Miss Smith too. She'll take you."

This time Jane glanced at the nurse. The latter was apparently immersed in her book, but her eyes weren't moving. "You mean you're not going?" Jane asked Mrs. Berquist.

"I have my job at the hospital today. Besides I wasn't invited."

"Well, in that case—would you mind if I refused? I don't fee—"

"Oh no!" Mrs. Berquist exclaimed. "It never occurred— I told her you'd love it." She sounded genuinely upset, perhaps because of the embarrassment of calling back, or perhaps because she herself had to go out and disliked leaving her guest.

"Never mind," Jane said slowly. It was absurd to refuse simply because of a—an evanescence? A sensation? "I'll go."

"Good," Mrs. Berquist said with relief. "I'm sure you'll enjoy it. Miss Smith, perhaps you'd better get Miss Wallcutt ready. I'd better hurry. I'm pretty late—" She bustled off, leaving them alone. Jane stared bleakly at her lap as Miss Smith put down the book and got to her feet.

She was being staked out, Jane thought again, tied to the tree near the drinking pool. While the hunters waited for the big game.

21

She had always enjoyed fashion shows, she told herself (not sure how she knew this); then why was this one so unpleasant? It wasn't the fault of the clothing, which was a wild collection of patio pajamas, shifts, and swim suits which she liked, but of the people. Ellis Hamden's friends were polite but distant. They seemed determined not to be offensive, but nothing more. They answered her questions, but never addressed a remark to her, and when they did speak, their eyes never met hers. Where had she read that when the jury brought in a verdict of guilty they never looked at the defendant?

Miss Smith, in a starched white uniform, sat beside her, talking to no one. She seemed equally disinterested in the food and clothing. Her presence was like a palpable weight dragging on Jane's spirits. She had never supposed that a luncheon engagement could be so depressing.

Outdoors, she could see a bright terrace surrounded by daffodils, and in the distance, people playing golf. The pool was still empty, but evidently had just been painted, and it shone a vivid green in the sunlight.

What was wrong with her? Was she doomed to despondency for the rest of her life?

"I don't believe Miss Wallcutt wants to leave."

"What? Oh? I'm sorry. I didn't realize—" It was Ellis Hamden who had spoken. The women were all standing, saying goodbye to friends, collecting cigarette packs and gloves. She put on her suit jacket, and Miss Smith began wheeling her out. "Thank you so much," she said to her hostess. "I enjoyed it tremendously."

"I'll walk back to the house with you."

"Oh—that's unnecessary. I'm sure you'd like to play golf or—"

"It's too late. Besides I haven't made any arrangements for it."

The two women got the wheel chair down the steps and began pushing it along the driveway. There were cars all around them, women backing out and maneuvering to get out of the parking lot. She felt terribly hot, and the breeze was too warm to cool her. Again she removed the jacket.

"Would you like to walk around and look at the club?" Ellis asked politely.

"No, thank you. I feel a bit tired."

"Of course. We'll go straight back."

Unexpectedly Miss Smith said, "I would love to look at the pool. It's such a pretty one."

"There's no water in it," Jane pointed out.

"I just want to see what it's like."

"I prefer to go straight back, Miss Smith."

Gently Ellis interfered. "It won't take a minute."

Feeling ridiculous, not even admitting to herself the fear that was making her stubborn, Jane said, "I would really like to go straight back, please."

"Very well," Miss Smith said pleasantly. "Perhaps I can see it another time."

Jane, who had expected more of a fight, glanced at her in surprise. As she looked up, she caught an exchange of glances between the two women. She felt puzzled instead of relieved, as though she had done something they expected her to do. You're sick, she told herself. She couldn't have it both ways—that the suggestion that she view the pool was part of a plot, and the fact that they gave in so easily was also part of a plot.

Most of the cars had driven off by now. They passed within hailing distance of two men who were playing golf and then an unnatural quiet descended on the flat countryside. She became aware of the crickets and some unrecognizable birdcalls. As they approached the highway, she caught a gleam of chromium among the bushes on the other side of the road, and she wondered why a car was parked there.

Again not consciously admitting fear, she nevertheless found her hands tightening on the arms of the chair, and she couldn't stop the thumping of the artery in her neck. She was afraid they would notice, but they were getting on very well discussing gardens. Jane felt like an elderly, faintly senile patient whom people never included in their conversations. A car swept by and she noticed the rate of speed. It was a straight stretch of road and the car appeared to be doing about sixty. On the road they seemed to be walking quite near the macadam instead of the shoulder on the side. Turning nervously to see if the parked car was still there, she was distracted by the sight of another figure walking down the club driveway. "I think we're too far out," she said.

"What?"

"We seem to be quite far out on the road."

"It's hard to push the chair on the soft dirt," Miss Smith said patiently, and went on with her discussion.

Jane turned again as she heard another car behind them. Miss Smith and Ellis Hamden paid no attention to it. The car approached at a fantastic rate of speed, the motor roared and then the car swept by. Jane noticed that her knuckles were white and she opened her hands. I've got to be ready to jump, she told herself. And immediately afterwards came the censor, telling her she was sick.

The woman on the driveway was crossing the road now, and from the distance Jane saw her head toward the car parked in the bushes. She wore a cotton dress and sweater, and a scarf on her hair. Probably a golfer. Since she hadn't known when the game would end, and afraid she would get stuck by the luncheon crowd cars, she had parked across the road. Jane was so busy explaining the woman to herself she didn't hear the distant purr of another car. In the meantime the scarved woman got into her car, started it up, and waited for the approaching car to pass.

The new one was coming on fast, Jane noticed, a trifle too late. At that moment Miss Smith gave an exclamation, as though she had stumbled, and suddenly, Jane's chair spun out toward the road, straight in the path of the approaching car. In spite of all her suspicions, she was totally unprepared to help herself. She screamed and clutched the arms of the chair instead of jumping as she had planned.

She heard the ear-splitting crash, waited for the shock of impact, and felt nothing except herself skidding straight across the road. She turned, bewildered, and completely confused, and saw a scene that made no sense. The car which had been in the bushes was demolished. It was a pile of scrap metal, and remembering the woman, she screamed again.

The other car, the one which had been approaching so fast, had a smashed fender and was turned diagonally across the road. Apparently, however, the engine was undamaged, because as she watched, the motor roared back to life, and in a moment it was gone. All she could see was that the driver was blond.

She was in a state of shock. She couldn't understand what had happened. Then, completely bewildered, she caught sight of the woman in golfing clothes and scarf, picking herself up off the ground and brushing off her skirt. Calmly she approached Jane. "Are you all right?"

Jane was afraid she was going to faint. "Gladys—Gladys, how—what—"

"Bend your head forward."

"I'm—it's—all right. What happened?"

The other two were both talking at once. "I don't know what happened. I tripped over a stone and the chair got away—"

"How fortunate that Miss Valentine happened to be in the bushes. What quick thinking."

"I can't tell you how sorry I am. I simply lost control of the chair—"

"Don't think about it. It wasn't your fault. Anyway, it all turned out well. Miss Valentine, I must congratulate you on your quick—"

"What happened?" Jane repeated dazedly. She kept looking

from one to the other. Miss Smith was red and flustered, but Ellis Hamden was calm as she explained. "Your nurse tripped on a pebble. Fortunately Miss Valentine was just getting into her car and she saw that hit-and-run madman approaching. She started up her motor, jumped out, and sent her own car straight into the path of the other one so that it wouldn't hit you. Remarkable reflexes." Enthusiastically she turned to Gladys. "How did you happen to be in the bushes, Miss Valentine?"

Jane was afraid she was going to start laughing hysterically, but Gladys' matter-of-fact voice calmed her. "We'd better call the police and get a tow truck out here. We have to get out a description of the hit-and-run—"

"Oh—did you get the license number?" Ellis asked. "I'm afraid that I was too upset to notice."

"No," said Gladys. "I was sitting on the ground at the time."

"That's too bad," Miss Smith contributed. "I didn't see it either."

"How did you happen to be here?" Ellis persisted.

Gladys gave her a long hard stare and said, "I called the house this morning and the maid told me where Jane was."

"You called the house? How nice. I mean—don't you work? That is—then you *came* here? From the city?"

Slowly Gladys said, "I wanted to see how Jane was—that's why I called. I happen to be on vacation. That's why I wasn't at work. And I never said I lived in the city."

"Where do you live?"

Again Gladys stared at her. "It seems to me that we're wasting an awful lot of time while you get my life history, Mrs. Hamden. Why don't you just thank your lucky stars I was here and let it go at that?"

There was a short silence and then Ellis said, "Of course. We're all in your debt."

"Yes," Miss Smith said, her breathless voice at variance with her large bulk. "I'd never have forgiven myself if anything had happened to Miss Wallcutt."

Cars were beginning to stop. Heads popped out of windows and questions came flying from every direction. Gladys sent one of the men to contact the police and get the tow truck.

"Well," Ellis said briskly, "we'd better get Miss Wallcutt to bed. We don't want any emotional repercussions."

"Gladys will take me," Jane said. Her voice was flat and unemotional, and all danger of hysterical laughter was gone.

"We really mustn't impose," Miss Smith said. "Miss Valentine probably has other plans for her vacation—"

"I don't have a car," Gladys said dryly.

By now they had collected quite a crowd. They heard a police siren in the distance and in a moment two uniformed men were questioning Gladys. The latter suggested that they get Jane back to the house and talk there, and one of the policemen lifted her into the police car. Jane insisted that Gladys accompany her, and the nurse and Ellis walked back with the wheel chair.

The next few hours remained a complete jumble in Jane's mind. Although she was in an almost fuguelike state, she spoke rationally enough so that no one suspected her confusion. She had a muddled impression of questions, answers, milling strangers, Mrs. Berquist clucking with concern, telephones ringing, uniforms passing in front of her, all of it congealing into one large transparent globe from which she could stand apart and observe. Oddly enough, she wasn't aware of being tired.

At one point Miss Smith started to take her to bed and, unemphatically, she said, "No."

Something in her voice caught Miss Smith's attention. For once it held complete authority. "Now, Miss Wallcutt, you're upset. I'll give you something to calm your nerves—"

"You're fired."

"I'm—wh-what did you say?"

"Fired. Dismissed. Discharged."

"Now, Miss Wallcutt—" It was Ellis Hamden. "You're not yourself. Naturally. But don't blame Miss Smith for the accident. She couldn't help it. I saw exactly what happened, and I can assure you it wasn't her fault—"

"Would you please go away, Mrs. Hamden?" Had she really said that? The narrow, weasellike face surrounded by the dark, netted hair, had swum in front of her eyes for a moment and then it had bobbed away, lost in the crowd.

"How will you get along?" That had been Miss Smith again. "It isn't easy getting a new nurse at a moment's notice. You can't impose on Mrs. Berquist—"

"I'll help out." That had been Gladys, the one unmoving object in all that weaving tumult.

"But your job—"

"You forgot. I'm on vacation."

"You can't dismiss me at a moment's notice—"

"I'll give you a month's pay." And then Miss Smith too was submerged, swallowed by the passing throngs.

In her semisomnambulistic state, she came to a decision. She was going to disappear for a while so that no one could find her. Ignoring Mrs. Berquist's pleas, she told Gladys to rent a car and take her back to the hospital. She was going to pack her belongings, remain there only one night more, and take off in the morning with the only person she was sure she could trust— Gladys. Afterwards she would hire her own nurse-companion, a complete stranger.

"And what about Austin?"

The voice that had emerged from the turmoil stabbed her with pain. What *about* Austin? She didn't know. If he—but she couldn't use the first word that occurred to her—if he cared, he would wait until she recovered her memory. Until then she had to cut herself off from everyone—him, his family, the Smiths and the Hamdens, her guardian, the Dickinsons, everything and everyone she knew.

22

She had been searching for something. It was desperately important that she find it, and yet, for some reason, she had become disoriented and had stopped looking. Her mind was muddled, and instead of continuing with her quest, she had lain down in confusion and mistaken it for peace. The worst part of her negligence was that if she didn't find whatever it was immediately, it would be too late. Perhaps it was already too late. She knew that a terrible thing had happened to her brain, but she didn't know what it was.

A strange vision had invaded her drifting, cloudlike world: an amoebalike creature which kept separating into parts and then merging again. Something like Siamese twins, cut apart but refusing to remain that way. Hadn't she read somewhere that if Siamese twins were separated, one of them had to die?

What had happened? Had years passed or just a few hours? Was this the same day she had come back from the Berquists?

She had to hurry, get there before it was too late. Get where? Too late for what? Perhaps it was all a dream. There were so many times she wasn't sure if she were dreaming or remembering. The threads weaved in and out, forming a dim pattern, but as yet, only the individual components were visible, not the whole thing.

What was that smell?

Surely, long ago, she had smelled something like it. The thought made her afraid. It was connected with horror. She had to keep it back, ignore it, push it down as though shutting a trapdoor—while underneath, something writhed and slithered and grew larger and larger, trying to burst out.

Once, when she had been small, her father had been playing a game with her—no, how could that be? He had died when she

was only a few months old. Then it had been another man. And
she had tumbled off the couch and hit her head. Everything had
been cut off for a while. Her mother had thought she was nap-
ping, but actually she had been in a coma. She hadn't been able
to remember anything that had happened that morning when
she recovered consciousness.

It was the same way now. Only, instead of a morning, she had
lost a . . .

Her mind was full of cobwebs, clogged with useless incidents.
She could hear a cricket chirping outside her window. That
meant, yes, of course, she was back at the hospital. She would
leave tomorrow. Gladys was in the next room, and as soon as it
was daylight, they would pack and register under different names
somewhere, a place where the evil couldn't follow.

That is, if the evil wasn't in her own mind.

It was like walking through mists which occasionally swirled
and lifted, letting her catch a teasing outline of a picture.

What *was* that smell?

She started to get up and investigate, and then remembered
she couldn't walk. The world had no room for the weak, the
disturbed, the sickly. Survival of the fittest—another schoolgirl
phrase seen through the mists—surely the haze was getting
thinner. In any case, the phrase was untrue. Survival no longer
depended upon fitness. Civilization provided for the sickly, the
old, the abandoned young . . .

Sit on the trapdoor. Don't let the thought escape.

How dark it was. She couldn't see the outline of the window.
If only she could get up and draw the draperies. It was like being
buried alive.

Memories ebbed and flowed as though she were under water.
Everything was changing shape, fusing, swaying, moving, becoming formless or taking on queer, nondefinable substance.
Another relic of the past: She had been walking in the dark,
outdoors, in the summer—they had been camping, and she had
left the tent to go to the outhouse. But because it had been a

moonless, starless night, she had gotten lost. Stumbling in the dark, unable to find her way back, she had begun to run in senseless circles . . .

The smell, like a scent of evil, was growing stronger. Her throat felt constricted, and she was having difficulty with her breathing.

Still in a state of semiconsciousness, she heard an odd sound. A snap. As if someone had broken a twig. Then, another, followed by a whispering, yet crisp rustling, like rain on dry leaves. She wished it would go away. She was so tired. She wanted to go back to sleep, to drop into the womb of darkness.

The rustling continued and then it began to alternate with an incomprehensible sucking sound like air currents. Then came a steady sizzling, and suddenly, without warning, she was no longer blind. She could see a light.

It was on floor level, and it flickered unsteadily for an instant before shooting up.

Like a dream which seems to take years but actually flashes through the mind in the moment of awakening, the mists, the memories, and the somnolence exploded into fragments. Her scream blasted through the annex. "Fire! Gladys! Wake up! Fire!"

Why had it taken her so long? What had made her ignore the evidence of all her senses until it was too—no, it wasn't going to be too late. She wasn't going to die like this.

She screamed again and began thrashing on the bed. The room was filling with smoke, and her throat burned. The rustling had turned to a raging crackling that came from every direction at once. She couldn't lie here helplessly and be roasted alive. She had to get off, crawl—

The door to the hall was on fire, and in a moment the rug would catch. It had happened once before—some time, somewhere, long ago—then too she hadn't moved fast enough, and because of it, because of it—

She reached out wildly and sent the lamp crashing. Clutching the bedside table, she pulled herself to the edge of the bed and tumbled off, sheets and blankets tangled around her. She felt a stabbing pain in her back and then the terror obliterated it. The rug had caught. She wasn't going to make it. She was going to fail again and this time—

She was on her feet, running.

The French doors were locked. Behind her the whole room was in flames, and the fiery arms reached out and touched her cheek. She tore the draperies aside, and turning wildly, caught sight of the lamp on the floor. Her throat was like an oven as she picked up the brass base, buried her face in one shoulder and smashed at the glass. It shattered everywhere and the inrushing air made the flames shoot higher.

She stumbled out onto the grass, almost falling. Turning back to the torrid furnace behind her, she saw something through the crackling orange curtain.

Red hair, a body clothed in something green, lying sprawled out on the floor of the adjoining room. The red wasn't the color of hair. It was the color of blood.

She was still holding the lamp and she smashed wildly at the doors of Gladys' room. As the glass caved in, she was almost thrown back by the blaze. But with a strength that didn't seem possible, she ran in, grabbed the body and pulled it to the door. She had to lift it over the wooden frame, and the frenzied conflagration almost made her drop it and run, but she gave one last tug and they both tumbled out onto the grass.

She had a confused picture of the whole building turning into a torch. A figure in a white nightgown stood a short distance off watching and nodding idiotically. From the main house came the sound of running feet and voices shouting and then everything stopped. There was only blackness.

23

The sun was hot. While she had been dozing, it had moved from her chest to her legs, and she judged that it was late afternoon. Someone had put a hothouse arrangement of yellow irises and white carnations in a vase on the table beside her bed, and the fragrance scented the whole room. Outside, the tree was studded with tiny green buds, but on the ground itself the fallen buds were crushed and bloody. She could hear the splashing ripple of a garden hose.

"How was I to know?" the man in the sport jacket and slacks was saying. "You must admit it sounded incredible."

At the beginning she had simply nodded while he talked, but he was confusing her more and more. She had no idea what was bothering him. Of course she knew she had been in some kind of a disaster, but she couldn't connect him with it. It was hard to think. Sometimes at night she would wake up drenched in sweat, still hearing the screams, the crashing of beams, the crackling of flames, but that was only a nightmare, wasn't it?

"Voices at night. A bullet. Killers in Cadillacs. Who could believe it? That reminds me. I have bad news for you. The body in Virginia—it was identified as Zee's."

What was he talking about? George used to say that if you don't understand something, shut up and listen. It was the only way to learn. Why "used to say"? He was probably still saying it. God, she was well rid of *him*.

"It was lucky you had Austin. I can't imagine what made him believe you—but he was convinced enough to hire a private detective. Did you know Gladys was a detective? She rented the gatehouse across the road so that she could keep a watch on you without making anyone suspicious. They didn't even tell *me* about it. I still don't understand why anyone should want to kill you. Maybe you and the police can figure it out when you're feeling stronger."

Was the man a lunatic or was she more confused than she knew?

"Even Miss Smith," he went on. "You were so right. Austin said she must have been recommended by someone named Hamden, but again, we don't know what she had against you. They knocked Gladys out, but they didn't bother about you. They were convinced you couldn't walk—and there must have been some personal malevolence involved. They wanted you to know what was happening."

"Did you say Hamden? Ellis Hamden?" It was the only part of his chatter that meant anything to her.

"Yes. We don't know who started the fire, but Gladys told the police that there was no doubt that she and the Smith woman pushed the chair del—"

"She was one of them. I heard them that night. I was outside the door—"

"What door? Wait. Do you remember something? Perhaps I'd better get the police—"

She sat up. "The police? They're here?"

"Certainly. They've been guarding you day and night."

"No one's allowed in," a brusque voice said outside the door.

"I want to give Miss Wallcutt a book on birds." It was a woman talking. Her accent was educated. Another woman, her voice decidedly queer, said, "My brother sent me a book. All burned. My bracelet, my letter. Big fire. My brother send me lots of things."

"Hey you—the gardener," the brusque voice said. "Clear these characters out of here."

The doctor got up. Going to the door, he said, "I'll take the book, Marlene." He came back and handed her a paperback with a picture of a cormorant on the cover. She stared at it blankly.

"Do you think you're ready to talk to the police?" he went on. "It would make things so much simpler if you could just remember. Of course I don't want you to push yourself. I'm sure in time—"

Time. She had been using time as though she owned it in infinite quantities. But the glass was emptying. She had to do something but she had no idea what it was. It lurked at the edge of her mind. When she turned toward it, it slipped away like a shy animal. While all the time, the grains of sand kept dropping . . .

"I suppose having a horrible thing like that happen twice will set you back. Austin told me that even picking up his sister's child sent you into shock—"

From the corner of her mind's eye, she could see it peering out, could sense the movement as it inched further into the open. If she were careful, if she went slowly, it wouldn't dart back into her subconscious again. Deliberately, cautiously, she made the effort, and there it was, out in the clearing, plain as the palpitating deer cornered at last by the hounds.

She sat up, her face so white he instinctively got to his feet. "Where's Dudley?" she whispered.

"Who?"

"Dudley!" The fool. Babbling incessantly and never saying anything.

"Who's Dudley?" How stupid he looked, mouth open, eyes blank.

She pressed both hands against her head to keep the fluttering thing imprisoned. Never make a scene. The most important dictum of her life. "Didn't they bring *him* here too?"

"There's no Dudley here."

"Isn't this a hospital—that is—I know it doesn't look much like one—"

The man's expression stopped her. Something new was dawning on his face. Then, slowly, exhaustedly, he let his breath out in one long, despairing sigh. He reached into his pocket, took out a handkerchief and ran it across his palm. "It's a sanitarium," he said carefully.

"Is it only for women?"

"What's wrong, Jane?"

"Jane! Who is Jane?"

He started to get up and then he sank down again. He put his face into his hands and nearly groaned aloud, but then he turned it into a cough. Finally he made himself sit up. He went to the door, looked out, changed his mind and came back. As though speaking to a third person, he said, "I'm out of my depth. I admit it. I'm way out of my depth."

"Please—I can't stand it any longer. I have to know. *Where is Dudley?*"

"Jane, do you know me at all?"

"I wish you wouldn't— I'm sorry, no, I don't."

"Dr. Stires? The name means nothing to you? The building— you're in the main building now. Do you recognize it?"

"Oh Lord." She clasped her hands as though she were praying and her mouth moved soundlessly. Suddenly she covered her eyes as though she had just caught sight of something unbearable. Her hands moved to her ears, and her head swayed back and forth on the pillow.

He went to her in alarm. "What is it? Are you in pain?" When she didn't answer, he went to the hall door and shouted, "Gillian! Gillian! Get my bag—wait—" Distracted, he glanced at her, called the policeman and dashed out. The policeman came to the door and stared at her helplessly. She kept writhing on the bed, her face contorted, as though she were in some inaccessible hell. "Oh—it was so—there shouldn't be things like that—I never could have believed—oh God, make me forget, make me forget. There couldn't be a God. He wouldn't allow—"

The doctor was back. Sitting on the bed, he tried to hold her hands, but they twisted away. "I'll have something for you in a minute. What do you want to forget? Forget what?"

"The people—the children screaming—"

"Yes," he said softly. "Tell me."

"The theater. It was hideous. You can't imagine. No one could imagine—"

"You remember the theater?"

"I wish I didn't. I wish I could forget. I wish I were dead. The curtain—a leg sticking out—it was moving. I heard someone— it was going through her—why didn't I die?"

"You'll feel better in a minute," he said, passing a hand across his face. "Just as soon as Gillian gets back—"

"Dudley!" Her voice rose. "Dudley!"

"Can't you do something?" the policeman asked.

"Tell that woman to hurry."

"I can't. I'm not supposed to leave her for a minute."

"Dudley!" Her voice was almost a scream. "You have to tell me. Where is he? Why won't you tell me?"

Desperately he said, "I wish I could. Try to hold on. You'll be all right in a minute."

"You're hiding something. I've got to know. He was with me. How could you get *me* out and not *him*? You've got to tell me. I don't want to live if—"

"He's probably fine," he babbled. "Naturally we don't know the names of all the survivors yet. But I'm sure he's fine."

"Where could he be? We've got to check—call the hospitals— I've got to find out—"

"What's going on?" It was Kirk, standing in the doorway, try- ing to see the thrashing figure on the bed.

"Kirk," the doctor said, "run. Tell Gillian to hurry."

Hesitating a moment, Kirk bit his lips. Finally he turned and ran.

"Take it easy, Jane." Beneath his hands, the doctor could feel the pressure building up within her. She was like an enclosed space filled with steam which would explode any moment.

"Let go of me. Let me up."

"Lie back. You'll be all right in a minute."

"I don't want to be all right. I can't waste any more **time. I've**

got so much to do—Dudley—it must be hours since—the hospitals
—and then the F.B.I. They have to know—"

He couldn't keep her down without knocking her out. Wetting his lips, he stepped back. The girl on the bed sat up and dangled her legs over the side. Then she stood carefully, holding on to the table and rocking with dizziness. He was unable to move, or to help her. Her face contorted with pain, she managed to walk across the room. "I have to get dressed," she said feverishly. "How my back hurts. I must have strained it when the balcony— Is there a telephone?" She was at the closet now and she opened the door. Frowning with frustration, she said, "These aren't my clothes. Where are my clothes?"

Uneasy, not knowing how to answer, he said tentatively, "They burned in the fire. You remember—"

"Well—you must mean the ones I was wearing—but didn't my mother bring me any?" Muttering, she looked down at the dressing gown she was wearing and then her eyes lit on the mirror over the chest of drawers.

Nearsightedly she bent over and squinted. The mirror was streaked and marred, and she had difficulty seeing herself. Finally she was nearly on top of it.

And then she screamed.

24

"But it's not me," she sobbed. "It's not me. What's happening? Oh God—what's happening?"

He had to push her down on the bed and hold her there to keep her from tearing at her face. She sobbed and struggled, trying to get free. "I must be out of my mind. Am I insane? Is this an insane asylum? Where's Dudley?"

"Lie still," the doctor panted. "If you don't stop this, I'm going to have to knock you out. Haven't you lost enough of your life?"

"I don't know what you're talking about. What's happening to me? Where—"

"You out there—is Gillian coming?"

"I don't see anybody," the policeman said.

"What's keeping that damned woman?"

"My face—how did it—please tell me what's happening."

"Take it easy," I said. "Calm down. I can't talk to you if you don't calm down, Jane."

"Stop calling me Jane." It was a scream, and then, as though ashamed of her outburst, she said more quietly, "I'm Reid. Reid Harris."

"Who—wh—what did you say?"

"God in heaven—what's the matter with you? What kind of a place is this? Where am I? Where's Dudley?"

"R-Reid Harris?"

"Didn't they get anything straight? I must have had my purse —identification—how long have I been here?"

He hesitated, eyes dazed, face spotty. As though she were undergoing a transformation from Jekyll to Hyde, he watched her in horror. "Look," he said desperately, "try to be calm. It'll save time. You want to find uh—Dudley, don't you? Then tell me everything. No, wait—I've got to make some calls—you out there,

watch her a minute." He ran out and the policeman came into
the room. The sight of her seemed to embarrass him and he
stared at the ceiling. Moving restlessly on the bed, she tried not
to moan. Suddenly she noticed how much farther the sun had
moved. It seemed to underline what the doctor had said about
saving time. Hearing an odd grunt from the doorway, she opened
her eyes. A strange creature stood there. "What's that?" she
asked in alarm.

"What? Oh—her. One of the patients. They call her Bonnie."

"Bonnie!" She couldn't suppress the moan. "How some mothers take a chance when they name their children."

"It sure is lucky you could get up and walk," the policeman
said, making conversation.

She stared at him. "I've been walking since the age of ten
months. Or so my mother informed me. Where *is* my mother?
Why isn't she here? Maybe she has Dudley. Why is it so warm?
And the buds—it's impossible. Buds in November. Or could we
be—is this the South?"

The policeman's eyes went back to the ceiling. Losing interest in her surroundings, she shut her eyes. Deep rings under
them made her look worn out, not from one experience, but from
centuries of misfortunes, stratified through the ages, as though
she could recall racial memories going back to her cave-dwelling
ancestors huddled together while the wind and the wild animals
howled beyond the range of the fire.

The doctor came back, breathing heavily. "They'll be here
soon. But maybe we can save time—tell me what you remember."

"I don't know why you keep harping on— Just find Dudley."

"It will make it easier to find him if you'll only talk."

"What do you want me to talk about?"

"Anything. Everything. Who you are—what happened—"

"I don't understand. You're not interested in the plot, just in
who I am—"

"What plot?"

"That's what I had on my mind. I couldn't concentrate on the play. I couldn't get matinée seats, so I got tickets for the evening performance—" She brushed something nonexistent off her face. "I didn't want him to miss the show. He'd been looking forward to it, and if I told them that afternoon, they would have kept me for hours, days maybe, asking me questions. Oh, if only we hadn't gone—if only—"

"Stop it. That's useless. Go on."

"It was for children—no, for adults too." She stopped, clutching at a tenuous memory, but it slid away. "They laughed so much—I missed half the lines because the children laughed so much . . . maybe my mother knows where Dud—"

"Go on."

"I smelled it. I could smell the smoke. If only I had grabbed him then—"

"Who is Dudley?"

For a moment she didn't stir. She seemed fascinated by an ant climbing up the wall. When she spoke, her voice was stiff as though she had packed it with some insulating material. "My little boy. He—he's four."

The doctor pinched his upper lip with his thumb and forefinger as though he wanted to hide his face from her. Then he rubbed the stubble on his chin and lifted his head. "Where—who is your husband?"

"I don't have a husband. I'm divorced. My mother—she kept warning me—she told me not to marry. Call my husband—exhusband. Maybe he has Dudley. Maybe he claimed him—"

"What's his name?"

"George Harris."

"The police will get him. What did you have on your mind? Why couldn't you concentrate on the play? Who were you going to tell what?"

"I heard them. The night before. My mother warned me. He got this mail all the time—pamphlets, odd organizations. Hate groups. God, how they could hate! I couldn't stand— But it was more than that—he wouldn't support us after the divorce. I needed money—for Dudley. I had to get him into a school, the neighborhood—you don't want to hear that. Oh, I'm so mixed up. I went to ask George for money—" Her face crimped in pain. "Call the police."

"I told you—"

"I mean—not police—government men—you know—"

"That's just who I called. Go on."

"I heard voices inside—George's friends. If anyone else had heard them, they would have laughed. It sounded like a joke. No one would believe—"

He leaned forward, his shoulders hunched and his hands clasped between his knees. "Yes?"

"They were plotting to kill someone. I was afraid. I felt like Bluebeard's wife."

"Who were they going to kill? Who was in the room?"

"Oh—my head—why does it hurt—it's like the time Daddy dropped me—"

"Yes, you fell. Tell me what you heard."

"You mentioned a name before. Ellis Hamden—"

"Yes," he said excitedly. "Go on."

"She was there. And this businessman, a friend of George's. He was chairman of the board of a big company. And I recognized another voice—I'd met him at somebody's house—a senator. A United States senator."

"A United States senator!" He swiveled to glance at the policeman, and as his attention left her, she sat up and cried, "*I want to see Dudley. Where is he?*"

She swayed dizzily and he caught her in time to keep her from falling off the bed. He pushed her back on the pillow and her eyes closed. At that moment they could hear a car motor and the doctor got to his feet in relief. "Gillian! She's got—"

He stopped as three men in business suits came out of the car simultaneously, each from a different door. The policeman went out to see who they were and the doctor heard something about "Barr—F.B.I."

As the men entered the room, he said, "There's a case of mistaken identity here. She says her name is Reid Harris. She's been telling me about a conversation she overheard among a United States senator, an executive in a large company, a woman—"

"Wait, doctor. I think we'd better get it from her."

"There's been some blunder. It's like a nightmare. She said her husband is—"

"George Harris." It was the same man. He got a chair and pulled it over to the bed. His face was pleasant and middle-aged, and his voice soothing. "Mrs. Harris, I'm Martin Barr. F.B.I."

"Oh." She shut her eyes. "I should have gone to you that same night."

"Yes, you should have."

"I wanted Dudley to see the show. Please—have you sent out an alarm— Do you have any news—"

"We're doing everything we can. Tell me about the conversation you overheard the night before the fire."

"How can I be sure you're from the F.B.I.? I mean—there were so many people I thought I could trust—"

He took out his wallet and held it up for her inspection. She stared at it dully. "Anyone can have cards made up," she said.

"Listen, Mrs. Harris, if I weren't from the F.B.I., how would I know about the letter you wrote us? You sent it the same day you went to the theater and you told us about a conversation you'd overheard. You see, Mrs. Harris, we thought you'd died in the fire. We questioned your husband, but he denied any knowledge of that conversation—"

"See, you admit it yourself—you told my husband about the letter—so anyone would know—"

"Mrs. Harris, would you believe the doctor? He was the one who just called us."

"Jane—I mean—they're the F.B.I. You can trust them."

She stared at them doubtfully. "What will happen now? If my husband—if his friends know what I told you—they may try to kill me. They might try to harm Dudley—"

"Please trust us, Mrs. Harris. Tell us what you heard."

"Why should I? Oh God—you haven't even found Dudley yet. If he's, if he can't speak—you can identify him by the bracelet on his wrist. My father gave it to me when I was small, and I gave it to Dudley—"

"She was holding it when they found her," the doctor said. "I have it with some things of hers."

"Never mind that now. Tell us about the conversation you overheard, Mrs. Harris."

"They were plotting to kill someone. They didn't mention names. It was so incredible. They were—their voices were matter-of-fact, as though they were discussing a—a fox hunt. I couldn't hear all of it. I was outside the door—and I was terrified. They mentioned a South American they were paying to do it. They were going to give the money to his family if he didn't come out of it alive. He needed the money desperately for—oh—I don't remember. I tiptoed away. I knew if they found me— I didn't know what to do—"

"Didn't know what to do!" It was one of the other men, a younger one. The man Barr glanced at him and he subsided.

"Well—who would they believe? Me or a United States senator? It sounded so fantastic. They could deny everything and then afterwards—well—I've read stories—perhaps an accident would happen to Dudley—or—are you sure they're looking for him? Suppose George has him? I know it's his own son, but George is so peculiar—"

"We have men checking, Mrs. Harris. Remember, we've just learned your identity. Go on."

"I didn't even know who they were going to kill. Then, the next day—it was on television—the governor was shot—and they said a South American had done it. I knew. Even then—I kept hesitating. I told you—I was afraid. And then, finally, I decided I had to tell, but I didn't want Dudley to miss the show. I know it sounds crazy. He'd had so little fun in his short—" She stopped and took a deep breath. "So I wrote—so I wouldn't change my

mind—and I knew you'd contact me the next day—and I went
—I went to the show and Dudley—"

"See my bracelet," said a voice outside the door. "My brother
sent it. Bad fire. So many things burned. My brother said he'd
send me more—" The man who had exclaimed, "Didn't know
what to do," loosened his collar, said something under his breath,
and shut the door.

"There's been a mixup, Mrs. Harris," the man called Barr was
telling her gently. "You were badly burned. Another woman,
Jane Wallcutt, was identified as you. We thought you were dead.
You were found with her fiancé—he was evidently trying to help
you—and he must have had her purse, because it was tangled on
both your wrists. Your clothing was—destroyed. You both—well,
you were both dark-haired, about the same size—"

"My face—I thought—I think I'm going to fa—"

"Take it easy. We have to have the names of your relatives.
Of course we could get them elsewhere but it will save time.
Your family thinks you're dead—"

"My mother—yes, call her—maybe she has Dudley. Mrs.
Crowell Phillips—please call—" Before she was through, one of
the men had left.

"So that's why they wanted to kill her," the doctor was saying
dazedly. "The F.B.I. contacted them so they knew she'd overheard—and then they read about the Chinese coin in the paper
and began to suspect that there was a mixup in identity—"

Outside the door Marlene said, "I really must protest. All this
coming and going is upsetting my birds."

There was the sound of a car motor again and then a door
slamming and footsteps. A man knocked and the policeman
opened the door. The girl on the bed looked up, rubbing her
forehead, and then the gesture became frozen and she seemed
perplexed. She blinked, in an effort to clear her vision. The
newcomer went to the bed, and both the policeman and the
F.B.I. man closed in on him. But all he did was stop and look
down at her. "They said—the doctor called. Do you know me?"

"Oh—I feel so confused—I can't—"

"All right. Don't worry about it. I just came to see if there was anything I could do."

"Did we—I seem to—"

"May I talk to her alone?" he asked, turning to Barr, recognizing him as the man in authority.

"*No one* is talking to Mrs. Harris alone. Who are you?"

"I'm Austin Berquist. It's kind of hard to explain—"

"He's—he was Jane Wallcutt's fiancé," the doctor started, but then Kirk appeared in the doorway. "Doctor, Gillian said you wanted this—"

"Where the devil has she been?"

"She had to find your office nurse. She couldn't fill the hypodermic herself. Well, I'd better get back to my pansies—"

The girl on the bed was struggling up, trying to see past all the people around the bed. Blinking like someone who had been in solitary confinement for years, she pushed the doctor away. "Lie still," he snapped. "I'm going to—"

But impatiently she brushed him away, sitting up just as Kirk disappeared. "George!" she screamed. "It's George."

The doctor, the F.B.I. men, and Austin did nothing for a moment, and then as her hysteria mounted and she tried to get off the bed, several things happened at once. The doctor took her arm firmly in his hand, holding the hypodermic needle in the other, the F.B.I. men leaped for the door, and Austin smashed the syringe out of the doctor's hand.

25

The days flowed into one another like connected streams, their waters mingling and becoming interchangeable. The trees grew greener and more lush, the lawn became spotted with dandelions, and the weeds took over the flower beds. Visitors came in streams as her two lives merged, joining Jane Wallcutt and Reid Harris in a never-to-be-severed bond.

She knew she had to start thinking about her future. She was no longer worth thirteen million dollars, but her reason for living had died with a four-year-old boy she had once taken to a theater.

Doctors' faces, the smell of ether—it had been *his* birth she had been remembering. Not the other things.

"You've got to eat, Reid." This time her brain got it right. During the nightmare, she had spelled it "read" in her mind and not understood its significance.

He was with her again, the man with the remote, heavily lidded eyes. "There's no point in dying now. We've gone to too much trouble to keep you alive." There it was again, the wary, rationed kind of smile.

He would sit with her for hours at a time, occasionally reading, sometimes talking, and at intervals explaining again. How he had grabbed for the woman and the little boy on his left, how the little boy had been torn away, how he and the woman had gone down together, and how the case of mistaken identity had occurred. It hadn't been hard to confuse her with Jane Wallcutt, considering the similar backgrounds and speech patterns, the ordinary brown hair and eyes, the more or less similar figures.

"But I began to feel the difference almost from the beginning."

"How?" she would ask, not because she cared, but because his was the one presence that soothed her, he the only visitor who could serve as a catalyst for some process taking place deep within her. Her mother had been too scarred by what had happened.

"Well—on the superficial level, there were certainly enough indications. For one thing, you didn't smoke and Jane smoked incessantly."

Jane again. She would have to carry her around for the rest of her life.

"For another—you preferred rum punch to martinis."

"On what ephemeral things our identities depend!"

"Oh, they were just guideposts. Like the fact that you were nearsighted. But there were more important indic—"

"Why didn't you go to the police?"

"It's hard to say. Maybe I didn't want them to arrest you. Besides, they would laugh at evidence like smoking and preference in drinks. And they would discount the important evidence."

"What was the important evidence?

"The fact that my hormones reacted differently to you than they did to Jane."

She would mull over that, trying to assess what he had meant. Then, leaving it to another time, she would ask, "How did you know he had tampered with the hypodermic needle?"

"I didn't. It all happened so fast. But when you shouted George, I realized something was wrong. Since he was the one who had brought in the syringe, I decided to be on the safe side. It was instinctive. What I don't understand is why your Dr. Stires never realized that he wasn't an epileptic."

"Dr. Stires never examined him. He inherited this place, and it's a home for incurables, not a hospital. He took me in because his family had known Howard Chalmers. And when George read about the Chinese coin in my hand and realized—or suspected—what might have happened, he had Ellis Hamden pretend to be a relative and bring him here. The fact that he promised to do the gardening was a strong incentive to the doctor, since he had a hard time keeping help this far out in the country."

Occasionally they discussed the progress of the trial. In Austin's opinion there would be years of appeals, and in the end the public would lose interest, and perhaps only a few of the lesser fish would be indicted. There was no evidence linking the assassin of the governor with Zee's murder; the note Reid had taken from Bonnie had disappeared; and although George Harris would probably go to jail for his attempt on Reid's life, if he didn't talk the others would be immune. And the legislation the governor had promised—legislation which would have threatened huge fortunes—would lie dormant, at least until another man, with the governor's convictions, appeared.

And then back to the personal:

"I felt there was something different about you the first day you were able to speak coherently. It did occur to me that the accident might have changed you—but, well, as I said, it was your whole chemistry. You were quieter—your eyes, well, the fire could have accounted for the haunted look, but still—of course I never saw you stand so I didn't realize that you were slightly shorter. But as I said, it was nothing physical that bothered me. Unless you could call that first kiss—" He stopped, and to fill the silence, she recited:

> "Say I'm weary, say I'm sad,
>   Say that health and wealth have missed me,
>   Say I'm growing old, but add,
> Jenny kissed me."

He moved from the chair to the edge of the bed and sat looking down at her. She looked back, twinges of memory stirring, but when he emulated Mrs. Thomas Carlyle, it was only lightly, on the cheek. "And then, of course," he went on as though nothing had happened, "Jane never quoted anything, even silly verse. At first I thought you were a fortune hunter, but then, I'm not sure at what point, I began to believe you. Even when I hired

Gladys, I wasn't sure whether it was to spy on you or to protect you."

"Who will pay for Gladys' car and her medical expenses and everything?"

"The insurance company will take care of the car."

"And the medical expenses?"

He smiled. "Don't worry about it. I'll take it back in trade."

Oddly enough, she had no trouble understanding that one. Without thinking, she said, "Poor you. You could have had Jane Wallcutt and thirteen million dollars. Instead—" She broke off. In confusion, she changed the subject. "How did your mother know Ellis Hamden?"

"Don't get any ideas. My mother wasn't a member of their kookie organizations. They were in the same—I don't know what you'd call it—social circles—and they attended the same church, club, you know. The Smith woman must have called the Hamden woman and told her you'd been invited to my mother's house and that was when they planned 'the accident.'"

"Didn't you ever—it's all so hazy—I wonder if I'll ever remember that interval at all—did you ever see my handwriting?"

"No. You never made out a check. Miss Smith saw to that. And she also saw to it that the note you sent me wasn't mailed."

Sometimes she would examine herself for long moments at a time in the mirror. "Whatever am I going to do with another woman's face?"

"Well, you know, it's beginning to change. I mean, you have characteristic expressions that Jane never had. In any case you're stuck with it." And then, with elaborate matter-of-factness, "I'm not having you go through anything like that again. Besides, I can't afford it."

She would let the words wash over her. *He* couldn't afford it. *His* hormones reacted differently to her than they had to Jane. *He* was the one who had hired Gladys. It surely added up to something, but she was too tired to think about it.

Sometimes she would go to sleep while he was still there, and her breathing would be so shallow it would scarcely move the covers. He would get up to touch her wrist, to make sure she was still alive, and then, moving softly, he would sit down and watch her. The sun would disappear behind the rim of the world, turning the sky to orange-red and then to purple-blue; the night noises would begin to seep into the darkening room—the hoot of an owl, a frog in a distant marsh, the ubiquitous insects; and the long, healing process would continue.